Spells of Revenge & Requiem

HARLEY JANE ROSE

Published works by Harley Jane Rose:

TAROT UNDERWORLD SERIES
1: Spells of Tarot & Tragedy
2: Spells of Revenge & Requiem

Stay up to date on all the latest writings by Harley
Jane Rose by following on socials:
@HarleyJaneRose (TikTok, Instagram, Twitter)

SPELLS OF REVENGE & REQUIEM

HARLEY JANE ROSE

ISBN: 978-0-6486445-4-5

Cataloguing-in-Publication Data

Summary: Mackenzie goes to war against a magical underworld
society while she searches for her lost family.

First Edition: October 2024

Cover design © Jaqueline Kropmanns

To those who've been broken,
let it build you anew.
Let it make you unstoppable.

1: THE BIRTH OF THE FIGHTER

The martial arts gym was alive with noise.

Heavy thumps, grunts, and gasping breaths echoed off the concrete walls. Around the large space of the warehouse, participants of the HIIT class punched gloves and lifted hand-weights and stretched in pairs, working towards their exercise goals. Belongings lined the walls of the room, avoiding the foam mats that protected the floor from the sweat dropped by its hard-working occupants. The pungent smell of the sweat pervaded the area, no longer affecting those who'd been in its odor as the hour class grew close to its end. Winter cold leached into the room from the closed windows and shopfront door, despite the body heat inside the room.

The sun had set mere minutes before, but already the freeze of the outside world had plummeted the temperature of the poorly insulated warehouse-style gym. The class attendees seemed refreshed by the change though, more determined to stay warm and active as they worked their high-intensity boxing exercise.

Mackenzie's black gym leggings stuck to her damp skin, and her lilac tank top rode up her hip as she sprinted on the spot, the purple a good complement to her red-auburn hair even despite the sweat-darkened state of both. Usually hanging in tight ringlets, her hair fell flat, weighed down by the excessive perspiration. Strands that had snuck free from her high ponytail were now stuck tightly to the back of her neck, and she fought all her immediate impulses to try and pull it away. *It will only end up there again in a few seconds*, she reminded herself.

Mackenzie put her complaining muscles to work, cross-body punching into her partner Ashley's foam hand pads. The gym owner and instructor, Grant, called for three minutes remaining for their set and she knew she had to use the time wisely. Keeping the consistent momentum and speed in her punches up was agony for her body, but it was a kind she reveled in, knowing it would equate to greater physical strength later. That's what she craved, what she needed.

The cool air of the room weaved between the hot active bodies, reaching the back of her neck, chilling the stray wet strands there. Despite the fire in her muscles and molten heat in her veins, she shivered as the sensation radiated down her spine.

Pausing for a moment, unable to continue as she gulped down breaths, Mackenzie flexed her fingers as much as the boxing glove prisons she wore would allow. She was sure her hands were swimming in sweat inside the gloves, as though it would never leave her. Fighting the urge to once again move the wet strands of hair at the back of her neck, she pushed on with the set exercise.

Her vision tunneled to the boxing pads as she focused only on why she was here. It drove her and helped her power through the immense discomfort. All she could see was the goal, the pain, the reason to keep going. She refused to look back.

Her skin heated further as the anger of her past circumstances boiled her and she worked specifically to make sure it would never happen again. The loud commands of Grant were lost as everything else faded away, and she imagined the pads she punched were the faces of Amari and Teo.

Harder and harder, she pounded her fists until she wasn't sure how she had anything left to give.

She had to be stronger and better.

Somewhere in the world outside this room, her mother was alive and in the clutches of the Major Arcana.

Mackenzie had been searching incessantly since she'd been released from the hospital months ago. But she had no real way of finding her mother in order to mount a rescue attempt to get her back. She'd been researching possible places the Major Arcana could be hiding out, reading up in her journal, trying to find any other venues they might possess to hide hostages.

The search had not been fruitful and so while the Arcana lay low, Mackenzie had taken to improving her physical strength. She was resolute; she'd never experience the powerlessness that Teo had made her feel, ever again.

Her mouth dried at the memory. *Teo.* The name still held as much potency over her body now as it had just after it happened. She remembered how he'd magically incapacitated her through her emotions until all she felt was sick.

Her breath came shorter, her limbs tensed as though he was in the room, and her heart threatened to smash through her ribs and bounce away from her with how quickly it was beating.

Her hits on the pads came faster and harder as her vision darkened until she wasn't even paying attention to the pads anymore.

Teo had taken what he wanted from her and infiltrated and controlled her mind so that she couldn't have fought. He didn't have that ability anymore, but he had still been stronger than her when she'd fought him in the memorial park. He still could've taken whatever he wanted from her without the use of powers and choked the breath from her.

The anxiety of that knowledge was unbearable.

The only way she could remedy that feeling was classes like this.

A hiss of air escaped from Ashley's lips as they pulled into a grimace.

Mackenzie was yanked from her anguished mental spiral at the sound, bumbling apologies to her.

"Ashley, I'm so sorry. I got caught up in my head and I-" Mackenzie watched her new gym acquaintance lift a padded hand to wave off the apology.

Pulling her hands out of the foam, Ashley rolled the discomfort from her wrists, not meeting Mackenzie's eyes. Ashley's short blonde bob was greasy with sweat and her blue eyes were tired, unable to hide the pain as she winced through an attempt at a reassuring smile. "It's fine," Ashely mumbled, cutting Mackenzie off.

The profuse apologies still threatened to creep up Mackenzie's throat again, ready to bombard her workout buddy as guilt restricted her stomach.

Grant headed over to the two of them, aware of the scene that had unfolded, catching Mackenzie's wandering glance before she could avoid his questioning gaze. "Hey Ashley, this set's almost done. Why don't you go grab a drink and I'll finish this one up with Mackenzie for the remainder?" He moved beside Mackenzie, giving Ashley her escape.

With a sigh of disappointment in herself, Mackenzie turned to face Grant as she was left to explain herself to the gym owner. She opened her mouth, intending to spill more apologies, silenced only by Grant holding up his hands. He was already braced with padded shields at the ready to continue. He nodded for her to restart the exercise and - hesitantly at first - she obliged, only settling into the actions as she heard Grant's verbal prodding for more.

Grant shifted from side to side slightly on his tree-trunk muscled legs – a typical heavy-weight retired martial arts champion, gym owner, and teacher. Standing taller than everyone else in the room, he was the kind of person one expected to see as a security guard, using his monstrous biceps and pecs to scare off bad crowds without even lifting a finger – even though he was more than capable if he chose to. Every time he shifted it reminded her of that. His hair was buzz cut so short, Mackenzie wasn't sure if it was brown, blonde, or a mixture of the two. His face was a series of hard set lines, no matter how much he tried to smooth his facial features, suggesting he spent a great deal of time frowning. Despite his "tough guy" façade, he was a gentle human being underneath when he wanted to be with a lot of care for those who needed it. Mackenzie had been privy to a number of stories over the last few weeks that had given her a good sense of the full scope of volunteering work he'd done out of the goodness of his heart. It put her mind at ease to know there were still true selfless good people left in the world willing to look after the underdog.

"You can push harder than that! Come on, Mac! Only a minute left!" Grant barked encouragingly, breaking into the monotonous pattern she had begun settling into.

Sweat dripped down her back in uncomfortably fast flows as she responded to Grant's commands, cross-body punching faster and harder until the wetness along her skin made her feel as though she'd stepped into the shower.

"Duck!" Grant ordered quickly, as one of the gloved hands disappeared from range and swiped for her neck.

Dropping into a low squat, Mackenzie narrowly avoided the attack, adrenaline pumping through her, creating a hyper-awareness of Grant's movements and what his body might be broadcasting.

The pad returned to its default position where she'd

been initially punching it and Mackenzie resumed the exercise with new vigor. The destructive thoughts started to bubble up again though as her mind began to fall back into a monotonous pattern.

As though sensing her wandering mind, Grant gave one final swipe for her to dodge between punches.

The clock on the wall buzzed and the collective breath of relief from all the occupants of the room was audible. Some immediately moved for their bags, eager to head home quickly. Others meandered, making small talk with their friends and acquaintances. All found their exit at whatever pace their bodies could handle.

"Mac! Do you mind staying behind for a minute?" Grant called as she retreated in exhaustion to her gym bag.

Mackenzie didn't bother putting her jacket on, slipping the bag strap up onto her shoulder, and moved back to the center of the room. Waiting in silence, she watched while Grant farewelled the last of the stragglers making their way out the door. Cold air blew into the space in vicious bursts, the lack of people in the now-barren space evident by the bite on her bare shoulders. Mackenzie's skin prickled as the heat in her body disappeared rapidly.

"What did you want to talk about, Grant?" she asked as the hunk of a man turned to her.

"Are you okay?"

Mackenzie's neck heated in response, the warmth rising to her face as she dropped eye contact, her stomach twisting violently. Despite the concern she'd seen furrowing his face and her absolute lack of skill when it came to lying, she tried to feign innocence. "Why do you ask?" Her eyes widened in shock; she hoped he'd consider it too much effort to pry.

He didn't. "You know why. What's going on in that stressing brain of yours?"

"Would you believe it's just stress?" She smiled sheepishly, trying the new tactic of laughing it off.

He didn't play along, as though he could see through all her bullshit. "Nice try. What's wrong?"

"The same thing that was wrong weeks ago when I first signed up and you made a comment that I looked troubled by life. It's something I'm still not really comfortable talking about, but I appreciate your concern. I just got caught up in my thoughts today. I'm really sorry. It won't happen again, I promise," Mackenzie rambled, cursing herself as the words slipped from her mouth, knowing she wouldn't be able to guarantee it.

"Okay… Well, if you do need to talk to someone, I'm here. And if not me, I think you should at least confide in someone. Don't just bottle it up or it will happen again."

Mackenzie nodded, slowly contemplating. "I'll keep that in mind. Thanks, Grant."

"I've seen that look before, Mac, and if you don't address it, it will fester."

"The look?"

"It's the same haunted look that I saw on my wife's face when we met. It's the look of someone who has felt helpless and doesn't feel safe anymore."

Mackenzie's spine drew up straight and tense, as though she'd been electrified. Her mouth flopped open and shut as she floundered for any response, even just for a denial of what he'd said. The tight, twisting ball of guilt in her stomach went still and cold, an icy weight inside her, breath catching at the sensation.

How does he know? Is he a member of the Arcana? Have I put my physical security and trust in the wrong person again? Why did I let myself be alone with him?

As she contemplated whether she should stay and fight using her magic or see how far ahead she could make it if she ran, Grant interrupted her thoughts.

"Hey," he said, drawing her frenzied gaze as he clearly saw the way her face paled during her mental spiral. "I own and run a martial arts business. It's a common reason people start; it's something I need to know how to spot."

Mackenzie used her magical awareness, finally pushing out with the telepathic emotional powers she had spent months avoiding. She had to know the answers in Grant's feelings, though, and this was a way of being sure quickly.

Sifting through the mass of emotions that flooded her as she opened herself up to them, she felt towards the closest and strongest – the one nearest in proximity to her. Concern and worry broadcasted from Grant, warm and genuine in nature, a determination to make her feel at ease. She chose to believe it despite the small voice in the back of her mind that worried 'what if' her judgment was wrong: *What if I'm being played by an Arcana member?* Making sure she still had a number of steps between the two of them – to keep the voice of doubt in her mind content – she waited for Grant to continue speaking.

"And that's what I wanted to talk to you about," he drew her attention from her wandering mind that seemed adamant on focusing on potential dangers, stressing her out in the process.

"Hmm?"

"The membership you paid for includes access to the martial arts classes too, not just the HIIT classes you've been doing. I thought I'd let you know in case you wanted to give it a go. It might help you feel a little safer or more mentally secure if you tried one of those."

Mackenzie shrugged. "I glanced at them but didn't really recognize any of the styles. I haven't really had any experience with martial arts before."

"Then come give each a try and find out what works for you or what you like. They'll all keep your mind busier than this will and give you a sense of progress towards safety."

"I like the sound of that," she admitted, surprised by the words that slipped from her. A hint of a smile pulled her lips as she met his gaze and saw him catch the small gesture.

"Then I look forward to seeing you there, and hopefully we can get you out of that stressing head of yours." Grant smiled back warmly, and the tightness in her gut eased and softened slowly.

"Thanks, Grant. I mean it. It's a big help." Her smile widening until her winter-dried lips pulled painfully tight.

"No problem, Mac. We'll turn you into a pro fighter in no time. Then you can go kick the ass of whoever made you feel shit," Grant joked lightheartedly as he moved to the side, allowing her a clear pathway to the door.

Mackenzie laughed lightly along with him, all the while feeling how much happier the mental image of that made her.

2: THE FIGHTER'S RETREAT

The harsh cold air blasted into Mackenzie as she made her way out of the martial arts gym. It was a freezing reminder that she had forgotten to put her jacket on before she'd pushed through the door, a woman on a mission.

Mackenzie let the door clang open on its hinges before swinging shut behind her, the soft-close catching it before it could slam. She didn't bother to look back and check on it as she powered along with her newfound motivation and a renewed sense of life positivity.

Grant had reinvigorated her sense of self with the conversation, setting alight a powerful feeling in her she hadn't felt in some time, if ever. It was a warmth that blazed internally, warring against the icy temperature that pressed against her skin from the outside. The idea that she could defend herself against attackers physically - something she'd never been able to... It was something she hadn't realized she wanted or needed, but now that she knew it existed, it was at the forefront of her mind. The new goal.

She didn't bother to stop to pull her jacket out from her bag to put it on, excited to get home as quickly as possible and tell Kai all about her day. To tell him that regardless of the lack of progress she'd had searching for information on her mother, she was at least going to be improving her ability to defend herself physically against the Major Arcana, should they try to attack her. This time she could be prepared and no one would be getting the jump on her.

The wind was blowing gales as it pushed its way between the buildings on the main street Mackenzie hurried down. Warm scents of buttered pastries and greased hot food gusted in, punching through the chilly coastal air.

The further she moved down the main street, headed for home, the more she noticed the differences in her powers, now that she had released them again. For months she had kept them pushed down, unused since the night at the memorial park. The less she used it, the easier it had been to keep control over it, and not feel the touch of the unwanted power that only served as a sickening memory for something she wished to forget. Until now.

Once she had reached for it to secure her feelings of safety around Grant and finally pulled it free from its mental box, there was no returning it. It had been awoken.

A cacophony of emotions swarmed her from people in her radius, just safety inside the warm buildings on either side of her, unknowingly broadcasting themselves to her. The feelings begged to be heard – felt – varying from calm content happiness to jealousy, anger, stress, and everything in between, trying to shatter the powerful motivational emotions of Mackenzie's that pushed her home excitedly.

She knew she wasn't going to be able to shove it away this time - the control of her emotional awareness powers fading. The psychic noise was here to stay and it wasn't going to be contained this time.

Mackenzie lifted her chin, determined not to let other people's emotions ruin her powerful resolve, no matter how strongly they pushed on her emotional periphery.

She just had to make it home where it was less crowded and she could focus and learn how to control it from the comfort and security of her warm home, surrounded by Kai's caring, soothing feelings.

Reaching the corner, Mackenzie slipped down the side street she normally used, heading for the Salem Common, free from the wind and the chill for a moment before it found her again.

A door jingled as people moved outside to brave the cold, and a woman gave a melodious giggle across the road from her.

Turning her head to glimpse the pair that had joined the pavement opposite her on the road, Mackenzie glimpsed both the dark brown and orange hair pushed closely in soft, happy conversation. The feelings that reached her from them were nothing but contented and warm, and yet it stopped her heart, feet, and resolve in its tracks, freezing her like a statue.

Amari and Lily spoke quietly as they walked away from her on the other side of the road, totally oblivious to her presence as they laughed, hand in hand, rugged up in their winter clothing. Mackenzie's gaze followed them as they moved away, sure they would spot her at any point, but they continued on until they turned the corner onto the main street behind her.

Returning her attention back to the journey home, Mackenzie willed her body to work, stiffness holding her limbs in response. Only fear made her body move, her limbs so weak in their movements that she was sure her bones would crack and surrender her body to the pavement. Her heart fought to find a normal rhythm again.

Memories she'd fought to ignore, the stomach-consuming feeling of helplessness that accompanied it, swarmed her. Images of Amari slipping the knife into her abdomen, and the sharp warmth that robbed Mackenzie of all her strength before she had a moment to realize what was happening, replayed like a vivid waking dream. Her eyes stared unseeingly at the paved ground beneath her. Her lungs barely worked on instinct, somehow taking in air as her heart tried to kick itself into functioning like a broken engine she had to gun harder and harder just to get started again.

Leaning forward slightly, Mackenzie got her steps to work, moving closer to the Common again, hurrying for an entirely different reason now as the strong sense of power and security in her failed.

The magic she had little control over began to grow louder, ready to consume her mind with whatever it found. The noise was deafening, and as she reached up instinctively to cover her ears, she knew it wouldn't hold. Focusing on futile actions instead of plowing home would only serve to slow her down.

Just get home quickly, she ordered herself as her steps sped up.

Putting her head down against the wind blowing against her face, she trudged forward, ignoring the bite of the icy weather on her bare shoulders as the cacophony of telepathic emotions stole her focus. She knew none of it was her own – she could separate her own from the world around her, but it was still affecting her with the sheer volume and intensity of the world of emotions around her and she was quickly losing the ability to regulate it as her own fear and insecurity hijacked the show.

It wasn't a far trek to the Common and yet it felt like a marathon. Checking over her shoulder regularly to make sure Amari and Lily hadn't turned back on themselves and followed her to the park, Mackenzie could feel her unstable steps threatening to trip her if she landed her foot even slightly wrong. It was pure luck she was still standing and not on the ground with scraped knees and hands.

The sweat along Mackenzie's skin had well and truly cooled off and – at this temperature – she worried it was turning to ice. But the horrid weather against her bare arms did nothing to distract from the lack of progress she'd made finding her kidnapped mother or how truly unsafe she felt in the open, with a woman who had attempted to murder her walking around nearby with a smile on her face.

Not to mention how there were several members of the organization that wanted her dead wandering around in the town and any person could be one of them – and they knew who she was. The attack could come around *any* corner at *any* time from *any* stranger and it had severely hindered her ability to meet anyone in this town and carry on a conversation too long.

Can I even trust Grant? Any remaining semblance of power and security disappeared entirely as she questioned everything.

Lucy and Kai were the only ones she knew she could trust.

Focus on that. I have them. They're my rock, she reminded herself, trying to force herself to stay grounded and not lose it before she made it home.

Before this, Mackenzie had been lulled into a false sense of security, knowing the feeling could end at any point - but somehow, she hadn't expected it to happen today. Months without any hint of the Arcana other than what she tried to search for in her attempts to find her mother had made her comfortable when she really shouldn't have been.

Her inner demons had been unrelenting since the incident, ever the self-critic as they cursed her stupidity and the naivety that had gotten her in the position she was lucky to live through.

She had wanted to distract herself from the trauma processing of that and the lead-up to it with Teo by consuming herself with the search for her mother, but this time it had been a lot harder to escape. Besides Kai and Lucy fighting her toxic coping strategies at every turn – them not letting her fall into bad habits – the Arcana's presence had been surprisingly quiet.

Whenever Mackenzie remembered the calm that had settled over Salem, the hairs on her skin prickled and every muscle tightened aggressively, ready for someone to appear around the next corner.

Eventually she had accepted she wasn't going to see them – that they wanted to remain hidden. Until now…

Taking the dreaded steps onto the grass of the Common, Mackenzie forced herself to take breaths through tight lungs. She knew cutting through the park was the quickest way home with the cold and emotional onslaught, and she was more in danger from her own thoughts. She needed to be home and safe before she could soothe the inner voices and terrified internal turmoil of her body.

Everything about her was slipping and the oncoming brain-piercing migraine beginning behind her eye socket - thanks to the deafening onslaught - wasn't helping the situation.

Sneakers sinking into the lawn with each step, the blades of grass embraced her shoes as though they didn't want to let go of her. Her breath hitched, thinning even further until it seemed she were breathing through a straw as the gazebo proximity strangled her organs. Her heart was a nervous wreck, beating so quickly it hurt.

She forced herself step after step until she was finally moving past the structure, gulping air frantically, her lungs beginning to relax. Her stomach quivered and the hairs on her skin stood straight up and frozen, making her acutely aware of everything.

Shivers skittered up and down her spine that had nothing to do with the cold as the door to her traumatic memories threatened to burst open. A sensation akin to bugs crawling under her skin raced through her nerves, making her want to squeal in terror. Her mind settled on the memory of Teo's fingers, setting her skin alight with pleasure that wasn't hers, despite the repulsive physical sensations now overtaking her.

Think of something else, she ordered herself harshly.

Think of anything else.

Mackenzie knew how destructive her mind could get when she went down this memory lane – she had seen it happen repeatedly over the last few months when her mental discipline had slipped. And with the recent reappearance of Arcana members, she had fuel for the oncoming mental breakdown.

But the harder she tried to come up with another topic, the more the memories invaded her senses, swarming with emotions begging to be felt as strongly as the community around her. The cold surrounding her should've snapped her from her mental and magical spiral, but she was already too far gone.

Mackenzie's body was weakening, shaky as the adrenaline from her exercise subsided and stiffness began to set into her muscles. She glanced around to make sure no one else she worried about running into was nearby, worried her luck would run out and she would run into Teo now too.

Teo. She remembered the way he'd claimed her months ago and she had no choice but to follow along as warning bells and doubts were smothered by his magic. As she became his slave, feeling only what he wanted her to. Her body getting off on –

It wasn't real. It wasn't my fault. Remember that. He shouldn't have used his power like that, he knew what he was doing. It's not on me.

She knew the words were correct but she still felt sick and guilty at the memory.

The mental noise coming from the houses bordering the Common was deafening, she could tell one of the couples nearby was arguing by the back and forth flashes of anger and annoyance that reached her from the two. A squeal escaped her lips, not traveling far in the heaving wind and empty streets, as she tried not to push her hands to her ears, speed-walking through the park.

Tears welled in Mackenzie's eyes as she absent-mindedly traced the scar on her stomach, the sensation returning her mind to the memory of Amari trying to kill her and suddenly she was cursing her mind for once again being unable to escape traumatic memories.

Glancing behind one last time for mental security, she checked the space around the gazebo, thankful the area around it was empty. It didn't sate the paranoia though, knowing at any moment someone could climb out of its magical doorway hiding in the base.

Her breath shook as it slowed, the wind rattling every flimsy nerve and atom in her body. She felt weak. As though she were running out of time and she would eventually collapse in a puddle of immovability. She wanted to succumb to the darkness that taunted her; be a quitter, climb into her bed, and never escape.

She left the park, her feet touching down on the road on the other side of the Common, but the relief didn't reach her amidst the meltdown. The tears that had built in her gaze, blurring her vision, finally spilled down her cheeks. They chilled her skin, threatening to freeze partway through the journey to her jawline, but were replaced with fresh droplets before they could. It created a viciously cold cycle on her face that only made her feel even more pathetic than she already did. Sobs racked her throat.

Come on, she tried to tell herself uselessly. *I'm better than this.*

She barely made it to the front steps of the house that legally belonged to her because she was a failure. She'd been unable to find her mother and her mother had been declared dead.

But all along her mother had been in the clutches of the Major Arcana, and Mackenzie had never found her.

She'd let people convince her she was crazy for searching. She'd been right all along and she hadn't listened to her gut. She never should have given up…

Lifting her foot to the first step of the porch, a wave of light-headedness hit her, her knees buckling as she fell forward.

She managed to brace her fall with her hands, narrowly missing her forehead smacking into the wood of the porch as her knee caps were driven into the steps.

Not for the first time in the last several weeks, Mackenzie wondered how she was supposed to have control over her life, her powers, and her mental health. All three seemed to be full-time jobs and she wasn't sure how to get on top of it all. She was struggling to find the motivation to begin trying.

She sank her forehead to the ground between her splayed hands, resting it against the cool, smooth boards of the front porch. The smell of it so close to her senses as she closed her eyes reminded her of the forest walks back in Oregon, helping her take deep, slow breaths. The tears dripped off her nose and she worked to calm herself for a moment.

"You're not falling apart this time," she whispered. The words echoed close to her lips, like a secret between her and the house.

The front door she hadn't quite made it to creaked open noisily on its hinges above her. She didn't need to look up to know who it was as his fingers gently touched her back and the smell of his sandalwood cologne warmed her against the cold she had begun to feel. His love and concern reached her through her magic, giving her a grounding she could tether herself to as she blinked her eyes free of the flood of tears.

"Hey…" Kai said quietly as she lifted her head to see him crouching beside her. His gray-blue eyes watched her carefully, offering her a hand to help her up with an expression that said he hoped she'd take it.

Slipping her fingers in his, Mackenzie let him lead her up to standing, feeling how her knees twinged and ached. Falling into the steps in defeat was going to cost her for a time after, her knees stiffening tightly as the fluid rushed to them. She reached Kai's level, sliding her arms around his neck, not waiting to check in.

He didn't ask what had affected her so harshly or why she had collapsed. He simply rested his arms around her back, holding her close as she pressed her face into the crook of his neck. Her body welcomed his warmth, clinging to it like a lifeline.

Mackenzie's feet lifted, leaving the porch as Kai carried her in their embrace inside the front door and out of the cold. The warmth of his body heat pressed into hers was more of a comfort than the indoor protection from winter could provide. She could feel the calm he gave her, the ball of cold lead retreating and warming enough in his presence that she knew the meltdown was staved off for now.

She breathed in deeply, inhaling the smell of sandalwood, feeling his arms squeeze reassuringly around the small of her back as the front door shut and he walked them to the couch.

Without a word, she heaved her legs up and wrapped them loosely around his waist as they sat on the couch. She smiled to herself, her lips skimming lightly along his bare skin and she felt him shift slightly at the gesture. She sat on his lap on the couch, enjoying how their bodies melded together so perfectly.

"It's going to be okay…" he whispered in the silence and she stayed in his lap, clutching him and feeling his fingertips trace lightly up and down her back.

Finally, she lifted her face from his shoulder, loosening her arms but still resting them around his neck, leaning back. "I know it will," she admitted quietly, meeting his steady gaze. "It's just hard getting to a place where I'm okay with it all."

He nodded his understanding, tracing a finger up her spine over her tank top, still sending shivers dancing through her nerves. She straightened slightly, suppressing the contented moan that wanted to work its way out of her throat. "I just feel like I'm letting mom down by not being able to get over it all fast enough." Her voice cracked slightly as she thought of her mother and tried not to imagine the state she might be in.

"You know you don't have to *get over it all,* right? You're stronger than you realize but you're allowed to feel pain. The way I've always thought of it, you can either let it break you or you can let it make you anew. I know you think this is breaking you but it's not. You'll see the growth soon enough." One of his hands moved from her back to cup her cheek.

"You really think so?" A slight smile touched her lips, ridding her of some of the lumps in the back of her throat.

"I really do, Kenz. You've survived what would break most and I've seen your strength pick you up every time to push you further than you ever thought possible. You went up against the Arcana, you made it known you had their prized weapon and you're still here. You even made them go quiet for a few months!"

Kai's reassurance, while well-intentioned, made bile rise up Mackenzie's throat. The Arcana's absence – while good for trauma processing – didn't make her feel victorious, especially now that it was over.

"Or they're torturing mom to punish me," she muttered, dropping her eyes down between them.

"You can't think like that!" Kai lifted her gaze with a finger under the chin. "You're going to find her and rescue her. I know it. But don't be so determined to wallow in not being able to find her or I will bring in Lucy for the tough love."

Mackenzie sat back, her spine straight, almost falling off his lap at his words. His face was furrowed in determination, the hard lines of his expression were stubborn as he watched her process his words. And as she felt the unending love and concern in his emotional aura, she let the giggle burst from her. "You can't give the tough love?"

She watched his face soften at the sound. He returned her grin as his hand placed on her hips, just in case she leaned any further back and fell. "Not that kind, love," he said with a devilish grin as he pulled her closer until she could feel him pressed between her legs, the clothing barely separating them.

3: THE FIGHTER'S KISS

The sexual desire hung in the air between Kai and Mackenzie, the tension palpable in the silence. They kept their gazes connected, daring each other to move as the points where their bodies met heated, even through their clothing.

He moved one of his hands up, brushing a stray hair from her face. She smiled as his fingers lingered against her cheek. Before she could bite her lip and knowingly drive him wild, he spoke.

"Feeling a bit better?" He ran the tip of his finger over the top of her ear.

Mackenzie's breath relaxed in a contented sigh. Swallowing, she felt the buzz in her nerves all the way down the side of her neck, begging for more. "I always do with you," she said silkily, unable to help herself. She knew how corny she sounded, but watched the way he swallowed and his chin tightened, making her insides heat in response.

"I'm glad I could help." His hand sliding to rest up against her cheek, he moved forward and pressed a kiss against her forehead. "So, do I get to know what made you break down on the porch? If it's a person I might need to teach them a lesson about making you cry."

"Don't even joke about that!"

"Okay, I'll stop. But seriously, what happened?"

"A lot actually. I got in my head at HIIT but I came out feeling powerful and indestructible after a good conversation with the owner, Grant. It all came crashing down though when I saw Amari and Lily on my way home." Her voice shook as she stumbled over their names.

"Are you okay? Did they hurt you?" He searched her body visually, checking for any sign of injury.

"No, I don't think they saw me. But everything came back to me that I didn't want to remember."

"Do you want to talk about it or are you more in the mood for distraction?"

"A distraction, please?"

He nodded and her body melted in anticipation of the type of distraction she craved. But his mind and questions turned elsewhere. "What happened at the HIIT class?"

"I got in my head while boxing and Ashley wasn't prepared to deal with it, so Grant pulled me aside to chat about it after class."

"What did he say?"

"He suggested that I give the martial art classes a try."

"Because he saw potential in your boxing abilities?"

"No. Because he saw the look on my face and has apparently seen it before. He said it was the look of someone who was trying to feel safe."

Kai nodded again, as though processing Grant's words thoughtfully before smiling broadly. "The martial arts classes sound like a great idea."

"I think so too. I'm going to take him up on the invitation. I enjoyed the idea of being strong and powerful, which is why I left on a high from the conversation. And then I crashed because seeing those two reminded me how I'm not."

"You are strong, Kenz. But I also think you're afraid of moving on."

"Afraid?"

"Well, you can either stay in the pain you're in, or you have to face the mystery and unknown of future challenges. Like what to do about your mom and the Arcana…"

Mackenzie sat back, thinking about his words as she mulled them over in her mind, considering his view. "You really think I'm ready to face it?"

"I think you've been ready for a while now, you're just focused on what *was* when you could be looking at what *could be*. You have amazing willpower and if you wanted to, nothing could stop you. But you have to want to move on."

"I do."

"Then tomorrow, it begins."

"What begins?"

"You'll see," he said in a low, mysterious tone, making her insides clench in delight.

"Okay, so tomorrow. Why not today?"

"Because *today*, I need to show you how attracted to your strength I am." He grinned, slipping his hands around her body, tracing circles on her lower back.

Her back arched involuntarily under his touch, the muscles in her legs tightening around him. The nerves danced over her skin as she bit her lip, slowly and deliberately.

Kai gave up on holding himself back, meeting her lips with a fiery passion that communicated every ounce of love he had for her.

She kissed him back, pressing everything she had into the gesture as her arms and legs wrapped even tighter, getting as close as their position would allow.

Everything about him was real, raw, and scorching hot, and all of the energy poured into Mackenzie. She had no problem surrendering her body to him knowing their connection – her pleasure – was 100% authentic, 100% hers. She tried to claim his mouth, her teeth raking over his lips as her hips began to shift slightly, drawing their attention to the friction of clothing between them. It would tease him, she knew that, but it also made every ounce of her warm and moistened at the action too.

He pulled her shirt up over her head in one swift motion, tossing it in the corner of the room. His fingers were quick and nimble as he worked the clasp of her sports bra, then that too was discarded and her upper body was bared to him. One hand moved into her hair – holding the ponytail her hair had been muscled into – at its base, the other scooping under her ass cheek.

He pulled tightly on her hair, and she let her head drop back at the motion, exposing her neck and feeling his mouth dive upon it.

He kissed it - nipping occasionally - just hard enough to elicit gasps of surprise, before his tongue slid over it, calming the place of sweet agony. He trailed kisses down along her neck and further until he sucked her nipple strongly between his teeth.

Mackenzie cried out, the feeling of pain flickering for a moment before falling away to the distraction of his fingers under her sliding along the seam of her gym tights. Her back arched deeper as she moaned breathily and she gripped her legs around his waist tighter to stop from falling off the couch.

Sensing the barrier to relaxed enjoyment, Kai released her ponytail, grabbed onto the back of her thighs, and lifted her as he stood. Then he bent, driving them both to the floor smoothly, positioning himself above her. He pressed his lips to hers, passionate as he pressed the hard length of him – still restricted by his pants – against the thin fabric between her legs. She clutched him closer with her arms and legs, warmth collecting where his body met hers perfectly.

He was teasing her, taunting her – she knew that and as her impatience grew, needing to feel him inside her, a wicked idea occurred. She hooked her legs tighter and shifted one of her hips, rocking both their bodies, and rolling herself on top of him. She could feel his lips under hers, pulling up into a smile and excitement shot through her veins like electricity volts, enticing her to see how far she could take her dominance.

Following suit with a grin, she let her lips trail kisses down his neck, lifting the edges of his shirt and helping pull it up over his head as he sat up slightly. She threw it to the same corner where he had discarded her clothing. She made her movements slow and deliberate, making sure he noticed.

He watched her hungrily, waiting while she made her point. She knew he was humoring her as she temporarily dominated for now. Both of them knew it wouldn't last long, but her stomach skipped about with excited anxiety as she held the reins for as long as she could.

Mackenzie bit her lip, watching Kai track the movement, leaning closer to her in response. Her teasing began as she placed her hand on his chest, stilling him instantly.

His eyes flashed to hers, surprised, his nostrils flaring with impatience.

Gently, she pushed her palm, guiding him to lie back on the floor, enjoying how hot his skin was beneath her hand.

She followed him, leaning forward and pressing her breasts against his chest, the skin-to-skin contact making her insides ache to be filled. She kept teasing though, determined to see how far she could push him before he cared enough to take back the control.

Her lips moved from his neck, light and trailing down his body, feeling his abdomen tense the lower she moved until she arrived at the top of his pants. She glanced up at him, catching his eye where he'd lifted his head.

Just to see if he'd comply, she quickly reached up and guided him by his chin to lie back again. And then with flying fingers, she released him from his clothing prison.

She could hear how hoarse and heavy his breathing

became as she teased him with her mouth. It made her giddy with power as she slipped her mouth over his shaft, hearing how audibly it affected his breath. She halted herself randomly, enjoying his impatience as each rhythm she began to set brought him closer to the edge before she changed it on him again.

Again and again, she broke from it, feeling him buck under her as he got into it before she changed and slowed to the point she knew it was torturous for him.

"Please," he begged finally, his voice tight, bringing her attention up to the way his head tipped back and his abdomen tensed.

With a grin, she moved back up until her face was meeting his in a slow kiss. Smoothing her expression into a widened one of mock innocence, she checked in. "Hmm…where do you want me?" Mackenzie asked.

"Pants off and bring your hips up here," he said, commanding as he kept his gaze on her steady, surprising her with his orders.

If she didn't know him any better, she would've thought he was angry. But she could tell it was him working hard to hold in his passion. He wanted her to surrender to him but he was letting her have her moment.

There was no denying he was enjoying it, but she knew at any second he'd snap and be on her, unable to control himself. She just wanted to see it; everything in her danced with excited anticipation.

For a moment, she met his gaze, wondering if she should comply or fight back against his orders to test his control. She caved; she could concede slightly and still drive him wild.

Carefully, she slid her tights and underwear off, holding his gaze confidently. As though it didn't make her heart hiccup or every nerve under her skin come alive with awareness, following his request.

She returned to teasing him with her mouth in her new position, her tongue experimenting slowly, varying

27

rhythms to see how he'd react, twitch and pulse. She was hyper-aware of the way she was vulnerable to his touch at any second, her lower region bared to him, feeling how fragile her power was in this position.

And yet his hands lay lightly on the backs of her thighs that straddled either side of his torso, unmoving.

The anticipation made her wet, she was sure he could tell, his fingers on her thighs tightening ever so slightly.

As the impatience of the wait began to weigh on her, she let the sucking rhythms he liked go a bit longer each time before she pulled back, aware of how his moans and movements against her mouth made her drip on his chest and she knew the self-control holding him back was a ticking time bomb.

Gods, I want to see him lose it.

She smiled to herself as she pulled back once more, hearing his growl of frustration. Proud of herself and feeling cocky, she didn't notice until it was too late that the elbow of the arm holding her up buckled.

Falling forward, she caught herself as her torso almost hit the floor, the hard length of him pressing into her stomach.

He seized the opportunity of her slip-up and she knew she wasn't regaining control. His legs moved on top of her and locked her shoulders to the floor, unable to touch him or move herself.

He'd locked her in place. A surprised noise between a gasp and a breathy laugh left her lips as she tried uselessly to look at him. She could feel his amusement reach her through her magic. She lay in her shocked, gleeful surprise, waiting for whatever he planned to do next.

"Having trouble moving there, love?" he drawled as she felt one of his fingers slowly skimming up the back of her thigh.

"Where did you learn to do this?" she asked, her breath hitching as she tried to free her body, but besides tightening the leg and back muscles, he had her trapped.

The way he'd wanted - apparently - as his fingers began teasing her slick opening, drawing a breathy moan from her before she could stop herself.

She didn't want to give him the satisfaction of her noises, wanting to see how much she could resist. But he knew her body too well, knew exactly the ways and places to touch to build the pressure in her quickly.

When his fingers slipped inside, his hand teased her to tightness. He was at the perfect angle to press the spot in her that had her finding release.

She couldn't move as she screamed out, him chasing her release again and again. It was like he was testing her against the intensity of her organs that tumbled her over the cliff unendingly. She was at his full mercy as his fingers pounded the spot, spilling her desire all over his chest.

She wanted to beg for a pause to the intensity that made her squirm and cry out, and yet he chased it again and again as her body rippled, tightening and loosening like a dance of pleasure only he knew how to elicit from her. Every single moment of ecstasy was real and it made it all the more enjoyable for her, not an ounce of her stress able to reach her when it was just the two of them.

Before she could cave and plead for the intensity to end, he released her.

His own impatience showing, he rolled her, sliding out from under and coming over the top of her eagerly. With one of her legs hooked over his shoulder, he seated himself inside her, every inch of him filling her as she met his gaze.

Sweat clung to her face again, her breathing hard from the breathless scream on the tip of her tongue as he started pounding inside, drawing inadvertent cries from her throat.

"I learned my moves from martial arts. But I've used my powers for evil," he whispered in her ear. He raked his teeth on her earlobe. Her leg pressed up closer to her body as he pushed in again inch by inch, deliberate and teasing, with a wicked grin on his lip.

He kept his face far enough away, she could feel him taunting her as she tried to kiss him and he stayed just out of reach.

She tried to pretend it didn't affect her, gasping as he suddenly twitched inside her.

"I love your evil," she said breathily, her words spurring him on to return to his intense, rough speed until they both tumbled to their joined release.

4: THE FOOL'S NEW BEGINNING

The quiet of the bedroom was peaceful as Mackenzie lay in the bed, watching the ceiling. She was in her underwear, warmed by the comforter and radiator as she took deep, slow breaths. Her wild auburn hair had grown more dark red in the months of winter. Now washed and dry, it splayed out on her white pillow, creating a sea of red along the pillow's surface like a ringlet ocean.

This is it. Now I move on and we finally do what needs to be done, she said to herself resolutely. The idea of it no longer terrified her; instead, she could feel the sense of determination that had settled over her.

Mackenzie and Kai had made love on the floor of the living room and spent the night distracting themselves from the oncoming storm in their lives they could no longer avoid: the Major Arcana. She'd gone to bed early, knowing this would be the last day before she went back to the searches for her mother – albeit a bit different this time. She was determined, however, that she wouldn't fall numb to life the way she had previously. She wanted to take Kai's advice and let the trauma she'd endured make her anew. *Stronger.*

Tomorrow, she told herself. A New Year's promise that was a bit late, but a resolution she refused to back out of all the same.

Kai had slept over, seeing the change in her after they'd made love, a welcome, comforting presence as she readied her mind for action. She'd fallen asleep with him tracing patterns and words on her back and skin, letting her goosebumps and little hairs dance under his touch with a smile on her lips.

When she'd woken that morning to find him gone, there had been no panic in her heart. The scent of his sandalwood still clung to the bed, letting her wake up slowly, relaxed. She knew he'd probably gone to look after some errand, and her implicit trust in him over the last few months surprised even her. It made her smile to herself, knowing her chosen family had now grown by one person.

The door to her bedroom opened without a knock and she turned her head, expecting to find Kai returning. Blonde hair poked around the wood of the door and Lucy's blue eyes glistened as she smiled her greeting to Mackenzie.

"Hey! I didn't hear you come in last night." Mackenzie sat up, her face melding into a surprised smile.

"Yeah, my shift didn't end till late." Lucy nodded. "I just ran into Kai on his way out."

"Yeah?"

"He's gone to grab breakfast and has set us a task for the day. So get up, get dressed, and let's get started.

"Do I get to know what it is?"

"Not until you're dressed."

Mackenzie sighed. "Do I get to know how to dress for this task?"

"It's not important. We're not leaving the house."

"Okay." Mackenzie pulled herself up, climbing out from under the covers. She crossed the room to the closet, undeterred by her lack of clothing around Lucy – they'd been best friends for years, it was nothing she hadn't seen before.

"Do I want to ask about the marks?" Lucy asked, amusement in her tone, referring to the love bites down and along Mackenzie's body – ones that would have been hidden by her clothing normally.

"You do not." Mackenzie laughed as she chose her outfit quickly, collecting it and clean underwear in her arms, and headed past Lucy standing in the doorway. She pretended not to notice the raised eyebrows and suggestive smirk on Lucy's face as she got a closer look at the extent of the marks.

Mackenzie shut herself inside the bathroom with a final readying breath before she fully undressed herself and moved for the shower.

As she stood under the jet of hot water – that she slowly turned hotter – she let the last of her toxins spill down the drain. She imagined it taking her previous stressors and worries away until all that was left was her readiness for the day to come.

When Mackenzie was satisfied her skin was well and truly prickling under the scorching water, everything else burned away, she turned the water off and stepped out.

Slipping on clean underwear, sweatpants and a comfy shirt, she headed downstairs to see what her day had in store for her.

Lucy was in the living room. She had moved the lounge chairs so that they were close to the coffee table, facing each other on either side, and had already seated herself in one of them.

The curtains had been shut and the lamps switched on; the way the room had been hidden from the world outside made Mackenzie's hair stand up, her body tensing. As she tried to piece the puzzle together, filling in blanks, trying to contemplate what Lucy and she were tasked with in the house, her mouth dried.

That was when she caught sight of the book in Lucy's lap with the old engraving on its front cover: the witches' pentagram with a circle of symbols surrounding it – each representing a member of the Major Arcana.

A weight dropped in her gut like everything she'd eaten had now become a heavy stone, pulling her down into the floor.

"What's the task?" she asked flatly, having suspicions about the answer.

"To work at using and controlling the powers of the Fool bloodline," Lucy responded slowly, watching how her friend took the news.

Mackenzie didn't move from her place in the doorway, her feet unwilling to move and accept her fate. She'd expected a day of research on the Arcana or looking into the other members to see if she could try and identify who they were. But this was a curveball she hadn't expected Kai and Lucy to make her do – honestly, she had assumed she could ignore her new-found power forever. It didn't really seem important in the grand scheme of magics. She just didn't want *them* to have it.

She dropped her eyes to her now-fidgeting fingers, chewing her lip unrelentingly. She wasn't sure how to rationally deny Lucy, so she settled on questioning, hoping Lucy would drop the idea on her own. "Why would we do that and not just restart searching for mom?"

Lucy was silent for a moment, causing Mackenzie to look – even just to check Lucy had heard or was paying attention.

She had been, and Mackenzie could feel the disapproval in her friend's gaze as she surveyed her. "Mackenzie, do you believe the power of the Fool is evil?"

"No, it can be good or bad depending on the user, same with all the Major Arcana powers," Mackenzie answered, slowly stepping her way into the living room.

"Then do you believe *you're* evil?"

"No."

"Then why would the powers of the Fool not be an asset for good in your hands?" Lucy pushed, a hint of a smile gracing her lips.

"It just feels so invasive that it kind of scares me," Mackenzie admitted, hoping it would sway Lucy.

"That's because you've only seen it used in a certain way. The way you control it could be entirely different, but you won't know until you try."

"Luce… I'm really not sure about this. Why does Kai want me to do this so badly?"

"KZ, you're going up against a powerful organization that has an enormous amount of magic… You need every advantage you can get."

Mackenzie took the final steps and plonked down into the single-person couch chair opposite Lucy. Her gaze flickered back and forth for a few moments between Lucy's face and the book that lay in her lap.

"Have you looked inside this since that night at the memorial?"

Mackenzie knew why her friend asked, noting her wary gaze; she wanted to know if the book had given her any answers about her new magic. She'd been terrified to find out if she'd inherited the journal of the previous Fool. She feared reading Teo's words on a page about how he'd used his powers the way he had, how he justified it to himself or to his future descendants. It had chewed holes in her stomach and stilled her heart when she considered the prospect, unsure if the words would take away from her pain or add to it.

But now, it didn't affect her the way it used to – she was still apprehensive – but there was a determination not to be affected by Teo any further. And she hated to admit it, but Lucy was right. The Major Arcana had their claws in places she hadn't even begun to guess yet.

"No." She sighed defeatedly as she lifted her arms slowly and let her friend pass her the hefty book filled with even heavier information. Letting it rest on the tops of her thighs, she breathed deeply, her eyes never leaving the pentagram engraved on its front cover or the many symbols surrounding it. Initially only one had glimmered purple, now two did. She could guess that these symbols all represented the powers of the Major Arcana. Staring at the symbol, no longer lonesomely glowing, seeing it finally for what it was... Proof of the power her family had left for her was grounding. And now she possessed a new line's power as well, it was time to ensure those powers were finally used for good.

With a slow, deep breath, Mackenzie finally opened the book and faced the music.

The family tree on the first page was the same as it had always been, settling her stomach as she looked at the Magician bloodline on the page, branching up through the generations of unknown relatives. She forced herself to relax and as her body sunk slowly into the couch, she turned the page.

Lucy moved in Mackenzie's periphery, getting up with a nod of approval, drawing her attention for a moment. "While you get reacquainted with the new additions in the book, I'll make breakfast. Yell out if you need me, KZ, even if it's just moral support for certain pages." She walked out, leaving Mackenzie to the book that felt heavier than she'd ever felt it before.

Mackenzie observed the new family tree page with cold curiosity. The Fool's magical tree spread out before her, representing something very different to her than the previous tree. While the Magician bloodline ancestry displayed a long line of family she hadn't known she'd possessed, the Fool's was a line that had belonged to her ancestor originally, but had since become a series of strangers whom she didn't care for or know.

At the top of the page was Sarah Good's name, still visible despite being struck out and replaced by the name directly below it – signaling the moment she had transferred her powers out to the other families, who now possessed what had originally belonged to her family. The name underneath was unfamiliar and uninteresting to Mackenzie as she skimmed down over the generations of Fools since the transfer. At the base was the only name she knew: Teo. His name was struck out, the same as Sarah's had been, and underneath Mackenzie's name now glistened as though alive with purple molten ink.

She knew the pages between the Magician's power descriptions would detail the extent of the powers she now possessed and that there would be personalized entries from the descendants of the Magician line and the Fools.

There was only one thing in this book that made her heart start to race in panic and made everything in her tight.

That was the hurdle she had to deal with first.

If I get this out of the way, then there's no weight hanging over my head and I can learn about the powers more easily with nothing else stopping me. Just get past this first, she reasoned, forcing herself to take another deep breath and begin turning the pages towards the back of the book and two more recent entries.

As she flicked through, she noted the chronology of the book had stayed intact: Fool journal entries she didn't recognize were now littered amongst the Magician's ones that had comforted her previously.

Finally, she reached the pages she was looking for.

Teo's shorthand entries sat on the page, organized and clearly labeled by date. Her heart clanged in her chest as she stared at an entry, mustering the courage to read about his time with the Arcana after meeting her. She wanted to see what had been in his heart and mind when he'd met her, if he knew what he was truly taking from her.

If he possessed any semblance of conscience.

Looking through the dates, her pulse climbed the closer she got to her move-in date, glimpsing phrases in Teo's short, straight-forward entries that filled her with a sense of hope that maybe he wasn't some supervillain out to destroy the world. It did seem in the entries she spotted that he was trying to do good in the world.

Then she stilled.

The Arcana has found the Magician's heir. I can feel the air of the organization has changed since they found evidence of her hiding in a tiny town in Oregon. Stories had led them to believe she had been evacuated from the town since her mother Anne had been apprehended, but she has been hiding there all along.

They are sure she will come to Salem of her own volition with the acceptance of her college application. Time will tell if she can be convinced of the Major Arcana's good path.

***

My role in this has been made very clear. I must awaken her powers, regardless of willingness, and convince her to use her powers for the benefit of the Major Arcana. At any cost. They didn't provide consequences if I fail but I can tell failure is not an option.

***

I could feel her fear screaming through me as she awakened. Her emotions blasted through me stronger than anything I've felt. Mackenzie's magic is so much stronger than she realizes and more than the Arcana counted on, for sure. I don't want to do this anymore but I fear I may not have a choice. The Emperor will see to that.

I've done something I can never come back from and yet I wasn't in control. Am I still a rapist if I was being forced myself? I was a literal puppet tonight for the Emperor. It didn't matter that I wanted out. I'll never get out.

5: THE DECISION OF FATE

"You can't be serious!" Kai said, his voice struggling to stay at a regular volume since he'd returned to Mackenzie's house to hear her daring new plan.

She stood across from him in the living area, feeling his horrified frustration rolling off in waves, punching her in the gut with her magical awareness. "You know, as well as I do, that I am. You can sense lies for God's sake!" she replied, exasperated as his responding emotions pressed against her, louder and more insistent.

"So you've lost your mind!" he said, throwing his hands up and looking at the sky as though it would provide answers.

"I'm not crazy! Just try to follow my logic here!" Her neck heated as she tried to hold the angered shriek from leaking into her tone.

"There is no logic!" he fired back, his anger and raised voice finally summoning Lucy from where she was prepping meals in the kitchen.

She rushed in, still in her apron, splashed with whatever sauces she'd been working with in the kitchen – probably buffalo. "Woah! Where's the fire, lovebirds?" Lucy interjected before Mackenzie could yell the obscene words bubbling to the surface. Lucy stood between Kai and Mackenzie, hands raised in surrender, glancing back and forth as though she were sitting at center court for an exciting tennis match.

"Have you heard Mackenzie's dumb idea that's only going to get her killed or kidnapped?" Kai jumped in before words could leave Mackenzie's mouth again.

All attempts to explain her reasoning diplomatically or logically disappeared out the window. A scowl pulled her lips tight as she glared at Kai's obvious attempt to get Lucy on his side.

"No…" Lucy said slowly and softly, trying to encourage calm conversation as she observed the raging fire of emotions from both sides of where she stood. "What is it?"

Mackenzie took a deep breath, meeting Lucy's gaze, silently pleading with her to understand as she opened her mouth to calmly explain, despite the fury in her.

Kai beat her to voicing it though, drawing Lucy's gaze and causing Mackenzie to roll her eyes. "Mackenzie has decided she wants to go and meet with Teo."

"What the fuck, *why*?" Lucy gasped, turning in shock to her friend.

Finally, it was silent enough and the attention had focused on her to explain. "He has the answers I need," she said, ready to elaborate.

"As to why he *assaulted* you? I know! Because he's a dickhead who is lucky he's not dead," Kai growled, his fury at Teo graveling his voice as he spoke.

"Someone was controlling him, forcing him to use his powers on me! I need to know who and he's the only chance I have of finding that out!" Mackenzie refused to back down. It was the first lead she had, and it was Kai and Lucy's fault she'd even found it – she'd been perfectly content never checking those journal entries but here she was, needing answers to her brand-new burning questions.

"Kenz, even if he was being controlled for that, are you forgetting that he lured you away to get stabbed and he might have done that of his own volition?"

Mackenzie could tell Lucy was working through her

plan, trying to understand as her thoughtful gaze went deeper into the carpet, getting lost in the process.

"I haven't forgotten" Mackenzie said. "Which is why I was going to suggest Kai come with me, but he was so busy *calling me crazy* that he didn't stop to listen to that part," she hissed in Kai's direction, his face blanching at her words.

He fiddled with his tongue over the front of his teeth, not well hidden behind his lips. He drew back from her as he realized his quickness to judge her plan had him guessing incorrectly, and while the anger subsided from his expression, Mackenzie's did not. Crossing her arms, she focused her attention on Lucy, letting her cold fury block out his attempts to soften her as he felt the shame of his mistake.

"Oh!" Lucy exclaimed, relaxing entirely. "I think so long as you go with Kai and have back-up, it's not a bad plan. Still not a great one, but it's a possibility you'll get answers, so I understand you wanting to give it a shot."

"Maybe I'll go on my own just to spite him," Mackenzie said slyly to Lucy, pretending as though she couldn't see Kai over her friend's shoulder, trying to catch her gaze with his apologetic, pleading expression. In her periphery, she watched his muscles stiffen at her words and felt the fear push against her as he worried what she'd do in her anger. She wouldn't go without him – couldn't go and feel secure without him - but she wanted to make him sweat for a second as punishment for not trusting her.

"He's being an idiot man. Don't put your safety in jeopardy for that." Lucy glanced back at Kai's concerned expression, softening to appeal to her friend who was still feeling the heat of her temper. "I'll give you two some space."

As Lucy exited the room and returned to whatever she'd left unattended in the kitchen, Mackenzie dropped her gaze to the floor and Kai moved closer. His hands lightly touched her arms, waiting for her eyes to lift to his. She didn't want to feel her frustration quelled – which she knew she would - if she looked at his concerned face, feeling his softening guilt pressing in on her more and more.

"I'm sorry."

"You should have trusted me." She felt the flare of his guilt twinge stronger at her soft words as she tried not to give up yelling at him.

"I know. I'm sorry, but you know, as well as I do that it's not out of the realm of possibility for you to run off half-cocked to enact these plans on your own."

His words drew her gaze in surprise. Mackenzie could feel the top of her lip curl slightly in disgust as she searched his face to find him serious. "You really think I'm stupid enough to do it twice?"

"Asking me a direct question like that is a trap," he said before answering. "Yes."

"And why would I bother telling you the plan then?" She crossed her arms as she watched him reel to find an answer, the temper simmering in her once again.

"You know what? You're right. You did come to me about this and I judged you too quick." He surrendered. His eyes searched her expression as he relented, and despite wanting to rouse on him further, she could see the regret and sense the desire for the fight to end.

She wanted him to really understand he hadn't trusted her or her ability to change and improve, and how much it had hurt and angered her. But just like the very thing she wanted him to understand, she had to let him be capable of learning from his mistakes. She felt herself soften and sigh. "You did," she reiterated. Her arms uncrossed as she let him pull her in closer and closer until his arms enclosed her in a warm stable embrace, one she couldn't help but welcome as their bodies fit together so well.

"I'll be there to back you up if you believe asking him will help. I'm not going to like it. But I'll be there for you," he said quietly against the top of her head as the tips of his fingers ran the length of her spine over her hoodie.

The hairs on her skin tingled, nerves buzzing and racing in response, and yet calming her nervous system – her heart slowing, and her breath deepening as she sank further into him, until she was unsure how she didn't melt. "Thank you," she whispered as her face pressed into his shoulder. "Now I just have to find the address."

"I know it."

She drew her head back quickly, her arms still around his body, loosening enough to look up at his face.

His expression was a youthful kind of guilt like a child being caught with his hand in the cookie jar. As quickly as it had puckered his features though, it disappeared.

"You know his address?"

"I do. Long before you moved to Salem, I tried to infiltrate the Major Arcana too, tried to figure out what their ultimate plan was. All I got was that it included finding the next Magician and that it was bad news," he explained, his fingertip tracing over her elbow.

"That doesn't explain how you have Teo's address. I tried infiltration too and not once did we go to his house." Mackenzie watched as Kai's gaze dropped from her, carefully intent on where their bodies met, stomachs and hips still connected.

"We used to be friends – or at least I thought we were."

His words rattled through her, robbing her of breath as she forced her mind to try and comprehend the mental image of the two of them together. "What?"

"When I was trying to infiltrate the Arcana, Teo was the one who seemed the least objectionable to befriend. This is before Amari was awakened - for whichever tarot she represents - and I warmed up to him. He genuinely seemed either ignorant of the work the

Arcana was doing, or brainwashed enough to believe it was good. In my book, that didn't make him a bad person, just stupid. So I guess we were both duped by him."

Mackenzie moved back out of his arms, stepping away slowly, eyes unseeingly staring into space as her mind stumbled jarringly over his words. Sitting down on the couch behind him, she sank into its cushions. Sifting through her memories of what she'd observed about the two of them when she arrived in Salem, it finally all made sense. "That's why you two hated each other so savagely? Because you used to be friends?" She stared at the coffee table, zoned out as she remembered the hostility between them at the party the year before. She'd noted there was history between them at the time but it had been forgotten amongst all the magical chaos and the unsureness of knowing who she could really trust. Now it had come full circle.

"His assignment – the one that had made us hate each other – was finding you," he started, sitting beside her on the couch and letting his initial statement sink in before continuing. "I knew where you were – from being there as a child – and I knew it was something that needed to be kept secret. I couldn't be sure that what the Arcana wanted from the Magician was good, but Teo believed that along with all his other tasks - he was doing good work that was benefitting the world and society. He began the search but came up with nothing."

"So…what happened? What about that made you hate him?" Mackenzie could feel her impatience pressing on her like a physical weight, begging to be lifted.

"I'm getting there… He figured out that my parents were involved initially and that myself and the family friends, Trish and Declan, were the ones with the information he wanted. When I wouldn't talk he went after them. He thought I wouldn't find out, said that because the Arcana had given him permission, that it was okay. He found out the location my parents had traveled to all those years ago by using his powers on them. He made Trish feel so much pain that she told him what he wanted to know. He didn't seem to possess a conscience to question the Arcana. I intervened when I found out what he'd done. He handed over the information before I could get to him."

"Oh God, Kai! I had no idea!" Mackenzie's limbs shook as though it were recent events unfolding, the horror vibrating through her.

"I tortured him for it. I cut him over and over again until he felt even an inch of the pain he'd inflicted on her. The only difference was after I'd finished, he went back to the Arcana to be healed, but the same couldn't be said for Trish."

"What happened to Trish?" she dared to ask, watching Kai search the carpet for answers, feeling the waves of anguish come off him and chew through her stomach, as though his story were eating her up too.

"Trish ended up in a coma from what Teo did to her. She's been that way ever since."

Mackenzie's stomach, which had been churning, bottomed out. Everything in her went cold, and the hope that Teo was at all able to be saved drained away quickly. "I'm so sorry," Mackenzie breathed, lightly touching his arm as he hunched in on himself. His shoulder leaned into her hand and she could feel the way it all weighed on him, tiringly pressing down on her now too.

"I get that you might need answers and think Teo can provide them, but I don't want you to get your hopes up that he's *just* a puppet in this. He's a willing participant who hasn't questioned what that cult has taught him." Kai's eyes finally lifted from the carpet to meet her gaze. She noted the heavy bags under his eyes that seemed to weigh him down.

"Yeah, I guess the journal entries were misleading." She surrendered. "They made me think he was just naïve and being controlled by the Emperor."

"You might get some answers but just don't drop your guard is all I'm saying. And now we know that the Emperor powers are active, we just need to find who it is. Remember that they have the blood-control powers and we don't know the extent or limitations of that."

"Knowing there is a mysterious Arcana member out there who can control people by their blood is terrifying. Especially if they're willing to do that to one of their own as well."

He nodded slowly, agreeing with the terror that coursed through Mackenzie as she spoke. His inklings of fear also pressed in on her, amplifying what already existed in her.

"We'll go visit Teo tomorrow together. Today, we train you." His strong confidence quelled whispers of anything else in his emotional aura.

"On?" she asked, his claim of training throwing her into confusion as she reeled for a possible answer.

"The Fool's bloodline power," he replied matter-of-factly. "You have read up on how to use the power?"

"I didn't get that far…" Mackenzie admitted sheepishly. "I only read through the Teo journal entries. You know… get the worst out of the way first?"

"I understand that, but it's time to get across these powers and start using them," Kai said, turning his body towards her on the couch. "And study or not, it's time to start. I'll be the lab rat."

Mackenzie's blood froze in her veins. "You just told me about how Trish ended up in a coma from these powers, and now you want to put yourself in the firing line?"

He confidently and unwaveringly met her gaze. "I know you won't hurt me."

Mackenzie's chest tightened, her breath coming in unevenly as she tried unsuccessfully to force her body to take in more oxygen.

Kai's hand reached for her cheek, resting there as he

breathed deeply and obviously, indicating for her to follow suit. "You'd need a lot of ill intent to do that sort of damage, Kenz and I know you don't."

"Only if you're sure." She sighed, seeing the resolve steadfast in his eyes. She knew he was right and eventually, she would be convinced of that. She may as well push away the fear that held her back and begin her learning sooner.

She did possess an edge over the Arcana now, even if it wasn't quite an advantage… yet. She had two powers, where everyone else possessed one. She had regained two lines of power that had once belonged to her family. It *should* be intuitive to learn – like something she was born to do. Or at least that's what she was telling herself.

"I'm sure," he reiterated, sitting back to rest his spine against the arm of the couch as he studied her carefully.

Another deep breath and she was facing him, cross-legged on the couch as she struggled to find any comfortable position in its cushions. Mackenzie clasped her hands together, instantly picking at her cuticles as she concentrated on her magical awareness.

"First things first, how easy are you finding it to read emotions?"

Taking the hint, she closed her eyes for a moment, trying to shut her mind off to the other distractions and focus only on the emotions and sensations that begged for attention. In the kitchen, she could feel Lucy's flare of annoyance – at what, she couldn't tell; she only hoped it wasn't at her. In the distance, outside the house in a nearby lodging, was the feeling of stress, like a string at any moment would snap and the impact would send her tumbling like a domino. And then, there was Kai, the closest and loudest of all, full of warmth and softness she could only describe as endless love. Her lips pulled in a smile, unable to hide how his emotions filled her with joy, and she opened her eyes to meet Kai's finally.

A smile pulled his lips up wide and warm. There was no doubt, concern, or worry in his expression or emotional aura as he raised his eyebrow in question, reminding her that she was yet to give an answer.

"Too easy?" he pushed, as though he knew how easily she'd slipped into that part of her magic.

"It's getting *your* emotions to shut up, that's the challenge." Mackenzie lightly jabbed at his ribs with her hand.

He seized her wrist quickly, his smile morphing into a wicked grin. "Oh is it now?" he asked, and she could feel an edge to his emotions. The smoky hint of lust and horniness floated to her as he held firmly onto her limb, waiting to see her reaction to this slight change.

Mackenzie knew the blush was creeping into her cheeks, feeling the heat rush to the surface of her skin, flushing her neck and upper chest, wet collecting between her thighs.

His nostrils flared, as though he knew exactly the reaction he had created in her body. A moment later, he was clearing his throat as he spoke, breaking the lustful haze befalling them both. "Now it's time to influence."

Just like a bucket of cold water poured over her head, the spell of arousal left her. The physical injection of cortisol in her body had her heart rate skyrocketing, her spine straightened, and her lungs crushing themselves free of air.

"I can't, Kai. I can't rob you of that agency. I just…can't," she whispered breathlessly, stammering over the syllables.

"Then don't. Just lightly influence something we're not going to act on, like tiredness or happiness. Stay away from anything sexual and it will be okay. Don't overtake the emotion, just test it, making it a little more prominent… It's going to be okay."

Mackenzie could feel Kai's complete faith in her as she met his calming smile, reserved only for reassuring her, and she knew it would all be okay just like he told her. Taking a deep steadying breath and giving her lungs the air they desperately needed, she readied herself to face any challenge life had to throw at her with Kai and Lucy to support her.

6: THE LOST FOOL

The next morning, Mackenzie stood stiffly in front of the house Kai had begrudgingly led her to. It hadn't taken long from her home, a shorter time than she had expected, and not nearly long enough to mentally prepare herself for what she was about to do. The taste of her breakfast had long since turned rancid in her mouth as she imagined what she could possibly say to Teo – what he might have to say to her.

Kai had moved just behind her the whole way here, letting her dictate the pace of the journey. She knew he was wary of her emotional state, the alertness in his emotional aura spiking whenever she slowed her pace considerably.

They reached the house with the green-painted door and Mackenzie knew the words that would leave Kai's mouth before he even said it.

"This is it."

The green-painted door did nothing to make her feel at ease as her steps stilled and her body froze. It had always been a calming hue for her and yet despite even the forest green tinge, nothing subsided the frantic nature of her body. Every nerve buzzed like crawling bugs under the skin and her muscles stayed stuck in place.

Willing her feet to move closer, Mackenzie could feel the tightness in her body as though it might comply but didn't. All of her organs worked overtime as though she were running a marathon.

Her mouth was robbed of all moisture, her throat feeling like sandpaper as she fought to swallow and warm herself against the icy freeze in the wind. The air barely expanded her lungs enough to combat the stress in her system that was making her feel lighthearted. Instead, all her hydration focused on her hands, pooling in the palms. Every extremity felt like it was buzzing and her vision became a blur of green as her eyes zoned out, staring at the door that stood between her and the cause of months of anxiety.

Thought upon thought, emotion upon emotion, stacked up inside her until she was sure she'd explode.

"I don't know if I can do this… I know I have to… And I know this was my plan… and… and… this might be my only chance to get answers but… I… I…"

Kai placed his warm hand lightly on the small of her back and the comforting empathy from his emotional aura surrounded her, a concern muted by understanding that made breathing just a little easier.

Her vision refocused and her breaths grew deeper as she concentrated on the aura, wrapping herself up in a blanket of his emotion.

"You can. I'll be here the whole time to support you. *He can't and won't* hurt you, Kenzie." His words were like a whisper on the wind, soothing the tense muscles in her limbs. "Okay… Let's take this on together. One step at a time. Come on," he continued, his warm hand pressing carefully, a signal for her to begin movement.

Miraculously, her body complied with him. Every foot lifted felt like a great weight though, tiring her with each step. So heavy she feared that any moment she might fall through the sidewalk and into the center of the earth.

The soft shuffling impact of each step shuddered through every nerve inside her.

They stopped before the painted green door and for a

moment, Mackenzie contemplated if this was a good idea at all.

Kai reached forward. His knuckles rapped on the door, the echo of the knock ricocheting through her ears, rattling her mind.

It didn't take long for the noise inside to flurry into action and, sooner than Mackenzie could calm her hitching breath, the door opened.

A woman stood on the other side. Without question, Mackenzie knew it had to be Teo's mother. She had the same dark features, the shape to her face and eyes near identical. Mackenzie wasn't sure what features Teo had inherited from his father.

The woman's eyes widened as they swept and studied Mackenzie's face and figure in return, settling on her red hair and eyes.

"You look so much like your father," she said quietly, almost as though she were speaking to the air and not the person in front of her.

The words turned the blood in Mackenzie's veins to ice. It wasn't the words themselves that had shocked her – she had seen the photos of her parents and could see her own resemblance – it was the fact that they were uttered by a woman who may have contributed to his death. The Fool's powers had been passed down to Teo from her.

Something inside Mackenzie twisted up tightly, and the result was a coldness in her tone she had never heard leave her lips before. "So I've heard, but I wouldn't know. He is dead after all."

The shock that emanated off the woman was like a physical punch. Mackenzie welcomed it, thankful for the truly honest reaction from the woman. She waited to see if there was any regret or guilt, or if the woman would reel with her words, but as quickly as she'd reacted to the statement, Teo's mother composed herself. She became a calm mask of cold, mirroring Mackenzie's. The only facial expression Mackenzie could read now on the woman's smooth façade was a sense of curiosity, her eyebrows raised ever so slightly, as though she were waiting for Mackenzie to explain her presence on the front porch.

"I'm here to see Teo," Mackenzie said, her tone flat.

"What do you want with him?"

Mackenzie's annoyance shot out of her before she could control her mouth, like a flare of fire was shooting from deep within her. "That's none of your business!"

Leaning back in surprise, Teo's mother pressed her lips together tightly. Biting back whatever response seemed to be on the tip of her tongue, she turned her head and yelled behind herself into the house.

"Teo! You have visitors!"

Before Teo could appear at the doorway, his mother walked away with a final sneer at Mackenzie, whose scowl didn't leave her lips in return.

The other side of the doorway sat unoccupied and empty for enough time that Mackenzie wondered if anyone would even show. As she began to look around though, peeking inside, he appeared.

The familiar face that had haunted so many of her nightmares moved into view, seemingly unaware of the way everything inside her cringed with a fear that had festered in her too long already. She met his gaze as his eyes traced up the lengths of her body, lingering on her curves before finding her face. She pushed her awareness out, feeling her guts twist at the ooze of arousal mixed with flashes of confusion through his aura. But as quickly as she could sense the question in his emotions, it slipped from her magical grasp. He blinked away any quizzical squinting on his face as he took in both herself and Kai, waiting on the porch.

"Want to come in for a chat?" Teo stood aside, directing them both in with a wave of his arm to the sitting room inside, just off the main hall.

Mackenzie stepped forward, feeling the uneasiness slow her steps in hesitation. Something about Teo's minimal reactions to their presence made her feel like she'd eaten something rotten.

Kai followed behind her, audible enough to make her feel comfortable she wasn't alone with Teo.

She stood in the center of the room, watching Kai find a space leaning by the window, the winter sun casting his face in glorious light and dancing shadow.

Teo followed up behind them, taking a seat angled towards his visitors, his eyes fixed on Mackenzie. "What can I do for you, gorgeous?" he asked with a half smile. Her innards shriveled in response.

"Gorgeous?" Her lips curled up in a grimace. An overwhelming surge of rage reached her from Kai as his muscles stiffened in her periphery. She watched Teo's gaze clock the movement, his relaxed state tensing slightly, as he tried – unsuccessfully – to pretend Kai's presence didn't make him nervous. Mackenzie could feel it coming off him in waves.

Teo leaned away against the back of the couch, his arms stretched along it as though he expected women to sit on the couch under his winged arms. "I'm not allowed to appreciate beauty?" Teo posed, his drawling words hiding the uneasiness that pressed on her from his aura, making her nauseous.

Something about this whole scenario felt wrong, but she was still in the process of figuring out what about it felt worse than usual, distracted by how her powers affected her view of Teo. Her eyes flinched shut involuntarily as she studied his face, trying to find the ticks in his expression to match the feelings smashing her from her magical awareness that told her this was all an act. Surely he had to know she could sense it all.

Nothing gave away that he knew she could sense it.

The heavy pit forming inside Mackenzie's stomach became harder and harder to ignore.

"No," she said, scowling. "You're not."

"Because of your boyfriend?" Teo's eyes flicked to where Kai stood with his hands clasped together tightly, hatred in his gaze as he watched attentively in return.

And then she noticed what her instincts had been trying to tell her was wrong.

There was no animosity when he looked at Kai, not like the last times she'd seen them around each other, as though the years of hurt, betrayal and anger had faded from Teo – the grudge he'd been holding against the friend that had left the Arcana and 'betrayed' him was entirely forgotten.

Mackenzie's chest became tight as she felt the hope at her possibility of answers slipping away before she'd even been able to ask the questions. "Because I don't want you to," Mackenzie replied slowly, as though it were obvious. *Because it should have been.*

"Very well. What can I do for you?" Teo's arms dropped from the sofa as they crossed his chest, the image of a 'no-care' attitude on the surface that she knew was just a façade.

"I came to talk about what happened with us."

Teo's long blinks in response told her everything she needed to know, coupled with the spike of confusion that dared not show on his face. Something had been done to him – something that had robbed him of his memory.

"When?"

"A few months ago…" she replied, waiting to see if it jogged anything for him, hoping with everything in her it did.

"And what was that?"

"As if you don't know." She hoped this was a charade and not some sort of freak amnesia – that he was very good at pretending and just trying to throw her off the scent.

"No, please enlighten me."

Is this bullshit? Mackenzie couldn't help but wonder to herself, feeling her heart race. She wasn't sure if him not knowing what he'd done to her was better or worse, if she should remind him, or just walk out the door now.

"A few months ago when you…and I…" She cleared the lump in the back of her throat that threatened to break her voice. "Slept together… and how that ended up happening."

She could almost see the bravado take over his face as the hidden confusion in him turned to worry. Mackenzie assumed it was because he was finally realizing he was missing memories and didn't want to admit it, but she couldn't be sure.

"Ahh… Look, if I slept with you and ghosted you, I'm sorry. But bringing your boyfriend over here to convince him of something isn't ideal, and won't rectify what's been done. I don't know what you expect to get out of this."

Kai straightened like someone had shocked him, moving closer to Mackenzie as he watched Teo with surprise, the rage diffusing from him as he studied the man intensely. Neither he nor Mackenzie had expected the memory loss as even a remote possibility.

"No. I'm here to talk about the Arcana *pushing* you to do it," Mackenzie corrected, stabbing in the dark and monitoring his response carefully.

"The Arcana?" His face contorted sharply, looking at her as though she'd barked like a dog and expected him to understand it.

"Yes, the Major Arcana."

Still no recognition showed in his reaction, the confusion no longer hidden as she prodded, hard and obvious and screaming at her to be heard.

"What? Major Arcana… Like the section of the tarot cards?" His eyebrows furrowed as he stared at her, near laughing with confusion. It was clear he thought her the one who had no touch with reality.

The fear she'd had of Teo - the anxiety the thought of his presence had once brought her - vanished. Along with it went any hope that she might find the answers to where her mother was being kept or who had controlled him. The words written in his entry seemed so far removed from the lost man in front of her. As far as she could tell, when it came to his memory of the Arcana, the diary entries were now the last remains of it.

"Ahh…" she started, unsure what else to say or if she should. If she reminded him of what someone had clearly taken from his head, she feared what could become of his mind. *If he remembers what he's forgotten, will he break? If he can even remember at all and if someone had removed his memory for sinister purposes, what would be brought on this clueless man by remembering?*

"Look, gorgeous, if you're here to convince your boyfriend that cheating on him was fate and not your choice, then sure… you tell yourself what you need to. It's not really my belief and I think it'd be best if you kept me out of this."

"You really don't know who I am, do you?" she found herself asking, feeling the cumulative breath held between herself and Kai as she waited for Teo to admit the truth.

He didn't, instead his hands raised up defensively as though she would physically attack him if he said he didn't remember her. "No offense but remembering the names of my one-night stands isn't something I'm good at." He glanced again at Kai as though at any second the tension in the room would snap and he'd be fending one of his visitors off in a physical altercation.

The breath felt like it had been punched out of her as the last strands of hope evaporated. He had no memory of her, or the Arcana – much less her mother.

"I… understand," she whispered, watching him drop his hands as her body sagged in defeat. She forced herself to move before she could sink into the floor and get stuck there. Lifting herself from the couch slowly and dropping her gaze to the floor, she angled her body for the door.

Kai moved up close behind her, following her train of thought. "Sorry for the intrusion."

She started towards the front hall, exiting and taking with her the disappointment that only created a tightness in her stomach.

A hand lightly circling her wrist with a tug backward made her stop. Lifting her eyes, she felt her heart lurch as she saw Teo watching her, his hand holding onto her. "I'm sorry I couldn't be of more help to you," he said quietly, as though Kai wasn't standing right behind her. As though it were just the two of them. As though he somehow understood that there was more to her conversation, but just didn't know what. Like he genuinely was apologetic.

Shaking off his hand before she could question it any further, she nodded her acknowledgement and rushed out the door. Teo's house suffocated her. It was too hot, too tight, too much all at once and her steps quickened the closer she got to the door. Without another word to Teo, and sensing Kai's presence behind her, she flung open the front door and escaped out into the cold, enjoying the bite of the air in her skin and throat.

When she was sure the door behind her was shut, and Kai was right on her tail, she braced her hands on her knees and stared at the paved sidewalk.

Inhaling deeply, Mackenzie tried to absorb what had just happened – what was now out of reach, not feeling the air fill her enough as the nausea overtook her. Her head spun and even though her hands on her knees felt stable, she was sure at any second she would go headfirst into the sidewalk.

"What the fuck was that?" Kai breathed to no one in particular as he too thought over what had just happened, his shock mirroring her own.

It took a moment before she lifted her head to look at him, attempting to stand up straight, swaying slightly as her mind continued to reel for all possible answers to what had just happened. "There's no one in the Arcana with the power to mess with memory, is there?" she asked, knowing it was a long shot. She had access to the same information he did – the list of powers allocated to each of the Tarot at the front of her book – and she couldn't remember that as a power anyone possessed.

"No, there's no one with the power to remove memories." Looking as though he was racking his brain for a possible item of information he'd overlooked, he shook his head, the doubt disappearing from his aura the more he did so. Squaring his shoulders, he puffed up confidently.

Mackenzie, however, was still trying to figure out the possible ways this could have happened, musing aloud. "He was definitely missing his memory though."

"Now, I want you to know I don't think this is your fault, but it might have occurred as a side effect of your confrontation at the memorial. Maybe having him in your mind while he lost his powers wasn't healthy. Or maybe those bracelets have side effects we didn't know about that caused some brain issues."

"This is more than an *issue*, Kai. He doesn't remember anyone associated with the Major Arcana," she said with a quiet sharpness, very aware that they were standing in the open discussing this.

"We'll figure this out."

"I just lost the only lead I had to find out where they hid my mom. Also, possibly the only person who would be willing to tell me who in the Major Arcana has the Emperor's powers of blood control," she whispered, dropping her volume dramatically as she glanced around.

Kai's volume thankfully followed suit, putting her only mildly more at ease. "You'll find another lead, Kenz."

"And what if I don't?" Her own question spoken aloud, spurring her mind to panic. As though the air did nothing in her lungs, she sucked it in quicker and quicker until she was sure she could take off with the power of her breathing speed.

Kai gripped her shoulders, yanking her closer and

encircling her in his arms.

For a moment she wanted to fight, but the warmth of his chest and his steady heartbeat slowed her panic, holding the air in her lungs longer and deeper.

"It's going to be okay, Kenz. We *will* find answers. We *will* get her back," he whispered against her hair as he pressed his cheek to the top of her head and squeezed her tightly.

She might have complained about her inability to breathe if it hadn't stopped her hyperventilating entirely. His warm care and concern flooded the magical aura she could no longer ignore, forming into part of her like it had always belonged there.

She replayed his words again and again to reassure herself.

We will find her. We will get her back.

7: THE WARNING BELL

The Fool
Current Family Name: Harris
Traits: Impulsivity, Innocence
Power Description: The Fool's power stems from their impulsivity and ability to react instinctively. The Fool's power is the ability to read and influence emotion, the range of which is only limited by the active user's capabilities and interpretation of said emotions.

The Magician
Current Family Name: Harris
Traits: Willpower, Creativity, Action
Power Description: One of the most elusive of the tarot, the Magician's power stems from the wielder's willpower and creativity. It relies on manifestation and manipulation and is only limited by the Magician's mind and imagination.

The living area was deathly quiet as Mackenzie stared at the book in her lap once again, the smell of old paper intruding upon her nose. Kai had long since left to go to work, helping as a laborer, and she knew he wouldn't be back for hours.

Lucy had also disappeared to work her casual job and despite Mackenzie knowing she had something she needed to work towards, she couldn't help feeling lazy.

Something about living off the money she'd inherited, now that she knew her mother wasn't in fact dead, felt dishonest. And yet whenever her brain considered the notion of getting a job, her throat constricted so tightly she thought she might die of suffocation.

She had no idea where or who the Arcana members were. The family names in the book clearly weren't the ones they used in public because according to every form of search and stalking, they didn't exist. She'd only just found out Teo's real surname had been Stilant, even though none of his social media or records anywhere had that listed as the name. *How am I supposed to find people surviving under fake names?*

It did add a whole new layer to it, especially considering everywhere she went, she'd been using her real name – now listed in everyone else's books as owner of both powers. If she wanted the element of surprise for her power stealing, it was gone now. Nothing about this situation felt fair and the more she realized about the Arcana powers and the convenient books of information she was now sure they all had, the huffier her breaths got.

The only silver lining she could find was the Magician's power – the one that had always belonged to her family that she'd first inherited. She smiled as she stared at the introduction entries on the Arcana list page, feeling the glee warm her. It was so broadly written, it meant – without the journal entries only for the eyes of the Magician that she possessed – the true extent of her powers wasn't known to the Arcana.

It was an edge, if nothing else. A way to be underestimated, and it had always been her family's.

Mackenzie had also tried to console herself, as she'd flicked through the book again, with the knowledge that she was the only family line with *more than one power.* The powers her ancestor Sarah Good had given out so willingly to others had started to return to her, and maybe with time, she could strip the Arcana of powers that were only doing evil in their wrong hands. They had been too powerful too long and their corrupted power had become unmatched.

It had to stop.

But first, she had to save her mother from whatever hell they were inflicting upon her.

The scribbling ink on the pages of the book turned into a blur as her mind swirled into overdrive. Questions, conspiracies, and possible places to look for a lead crowded her until she dropped her head back. Making contact with the back of the couch, she let her ponytail sink between the cushions, feeling the way it cupped her skull, while she let her mind whir away with its loud thoughts.

She'd spent hours pouring through each entry in the journal, learning everything she could about her newfound powers. Unlike her Magician skills, there wasn't much to discover in the way of special skills. It all seemed to be as discussed in the synopsis on the initial Arcana page – that or no one in Teo's family line had yet figured out how to wield the Fool for anything other than initially advertised.

The only new information she had been able to glean from the pages and pages of anecdotes had been the full damage the powers could do in certain hands. Victims of the power's misuse had died from brain aneurysms or had become braindead with very little life left to live. It was hard to admit, but it seemed her confrontation with Teo and the powers being involved had definitely caused the memory loss.

Now all that remained of Teo's Arcana knowledge and memory sat between the pages of the book nestled in her lap. And not a single word indicated her mother's location or who might know it. There was also no more evidence to indicate the identity of the Emperor.

Closing her eyes for a moment, she took a deep breath and pulled her head off the couch, shutting the book with a loud *clomp*. Stray specks of dust escaped from between the pieces of paper where they'd been hiding, flicking into Mackenzie's vision and forcing her to blink frantically as she set the hefty leatherbound aside.

Following her craving to snack, she pushed off the couch in the direction of the kitchen. The emotional stress of a nearby person approaching her house stopped her in her tracks. She couldn't see a window but she could feel the presence from the street move towards her front door, the feeling of chewing anxiety pressing on her as though it were almost her own. *Almost*.

She stood still, frozen as she waited to see if the stranger would think better of moving towards the house and leave.

Her nerves buzzed through her body as they inched closed. One step at a time, causing the anticipation to grate on Mackenzie as every painstaking fluctuation of feeling was broadcasted to her - hesitation, determination, sadness, anxiety and finally resolve.

Her feet remained in place, waiting even as the stranger made it only a few feet from her, on the other side of the door. She wanted to wait and see what they would do; no animosity or ill-intent that she could feel in their aura, but a guilt grew in them, overpowering their stress.

The knock on the door made Mackenzie jump. She could feel the whole whirlwind of emotion in the individual and had expected them not to go through with approaching her because of it.

She stood in the silence after the knock had stopped echoing through the room, contemplating if she should even answer it.

The knock came again, stronger this time as some of the guilt subsided to a calming surety.

With a deep breath, Mackenzie moved forward and glanced through the peephole to see the bob of near-black hair and tired blue eyes of Vicki on the other side of the heavy oak door. When she saw the familiar face of her neighbor and family friend, she unlocked and opened the door without hesitation. "Vicki, hi! I wasn't expecting you!"

"Well, I hadn't heard from you in so long, dear. I came to check on you and make sure you're okay,"

"I'm okay, I promise. I've just been… busy," she stammered, unsure of how to discuss the events of the past few months, unsure if she even should.

"Of course you have, but after your trip to the hospital not long ago for that awful stab wound, I just had to come visit. I'm sorry it took so long to check in." Concern flooded her emotional aura, the warmth of it pressing against Mackenzie comfortingly like a radiator in the cold.

Mackenzie couldn't help the soft smile at her worry, feeling loved by a woman who had barely any real contact with her. At the moment, Vicki was probably the closest thing Mackenzie had to family that wasn't Kai and Lucy. She couldn't bear the idea of burdening Vicki with her problems. "You, ah… know about that?"

"Of course I do! Salem's not that big, you know?" Vicki said, seeming concerned as she surveyed Mackenzie's body head to toe, relaxing as she noted her healed and standing. Mackenzie was hesitant on how to answer or discuss what had happened, but thankfully Vicki explained herself further, easing Mackenzie's confusion. "And I have a friend who happened to be one of your nurses in the hospital."

"Oh! It was just a little incident in the kitchen. Like I told the hospital staff, it was my own clumsiness with a knife while cooking. I'm sorry if I worried you!" Mackenzie rushed, her heart rate climbing in her chest as she lied to Vicki's face. It was exactly the lie they'd told the hospital when she'd been admitted, though. Kai, Lucy and her had all said the same thing and no one had called them out on the story.

Vicki, however, crossed her arms and furrowed her

brows as she watched Mackenzie carefully. "You don't need to lie to me, Mackenzie." she said flatly. "I know what really happened."

Mackenzie drew up straight. She wasn't sure if she should play dumb and pretend, in case Vicki was merely tricking her into admitting the lie. Maybe Vicki could spot the lie but didn't know the truth and wanted her to admit it?

"You do?" Mackenzie asked, her own face smoothing in confusion and mock innocence as her eyebrows shot up towards her hairline and she waited for any indication from Vicki that said she truly did know anything beyond the presence of untruth.

"Of course, and it was incredibly stupid of you to goad the Major Arcana. What did you think was going to happen?"

The words made Mackenzie feel the full temperature of the winter cold, as though there was no sweater to protect her and the icy wind froze her in place. Her muscles stiffened and the mock innocence fell from her expression like it had been slapped, her jaw loosening, unhinged.

As though remembering herself, she shook it off and moved out of the doorway, knowing this was not a conversation to have with Vicki outside the door. Sweeping her arm slowly in a daze, she watched as her mother's friend hurried past her into the house and made her way to the living area to find a free couch. Mackenzie watched Vicki note the Arcana book she'd left behind on the table; Vicki waited for Mackenzie to sit and talk before her gaze left its leather-bound cover.

"You know about the Major Arcana?" Mackenzie asked after a short stint of silence, noting Vicki's lack of surprise at the book's existence. She had seen it before.

"I do, and I can tell you they are not to be messed with. I tried to warn you away from them before," Vicki reprimanded like a mother warning her child that she shouldn't have eaten all the candy because they'd have a sugar crash.

It snapped Mackenzie out of her shocked daze, sparking the beginnings of frustration. "How was I supposed to avoid them when I didn't know who they were? I still don't know who they all are! Also, they kidnapped me for my activation… initiation… whatever it's called, in the first place."

"They aren't good people, Mackenzie. And once you're in bed with them, they are not an organization you can afford to cross," Vicki explained, ignoring the annoyed edge in Mackenzie's tone.

"How do you know all of this?"

"You don't think being best friends with your parents told me all I needed to know?" Mackenzie's silence as she thought of her own best friend, Lucy, was response enough for Vicki to sit back with a sigh. "This is not the life they would have wanted for you."

"I don't think there was ever going to be much of a choice where the Arcana was involved. Especially when I returned to Salem," Mackenzie said, finding her stomach dropping as she questioned whether she should ever have moved back to Salem. She knew the answer though – if she hadn't, she would have lived her life believing her mother dead. Now she had the ability to save her. She hoped.

"No, I suppose not," Vicki agreed, staring at the floor sadly.

Mackenzie's gut clenched as she looked at her mother's best friend, feeling her own guilt, wondering if she should tell her what she knew now about her mother. "So all this time you knew about the powers I'd inherit and you never thought to warn me?"

"Would you have believed me if I did?"

Mackenzie sucked her bottom lip into her mouth, contemplating, but she already knew the answer. Without any magic to prove it, she would have called her mother's friend crazy. She'd barely believed Teo and he had ways of showing her.

"Plus, I didn't want you chasing that. But I guess it was misguided of me, wasn't it?" Vicki continued with a small smile.

"It would seem so…" Mackenzie trailed off in agreement before considering her thought from before. "So you don't have magic?"

"No, and I wouldn't have wanted any. It always seems accompanied by trouble."

Mackenzie knew Vicki wasn't wrong as she thought of what her mother's association with a Magician had done to her, where being the mother of the next Magician heir had landed her. Mackenzie couldn't help staring at the book in front of her on the coffee table, wondering what her mother was enduring at that moment. "Yeah…" she agreed dazedly.

"Is something troubling you, Mackenzie?" Vicki intruded upon her thought spiral, drawing her gaze at the use of her name.

She couldn't lie to her mother's best friend. "There is. You and my mother were best friends, right?" she verified as though she needed to hear it again. She knew if it were Lucy and her, she would desperately want to know and so would Lucy. Vicki deserved to.

"Yes." Wariness drawled out each letter.

"Then there's something you need to know…"

"Oh?"

"My mom's still alive… The Arcana has her," Mackenzie said, watching Vicki as she broke the news, feeling no surprise in her emotional aura as the words left her mouth. "You knew?"

"They have been using that as blackmail against me for some time now. It was exactly why I couldn't tell you everything when you arrived here. The most I could tell you was that your parents had become involved with the wrong people, if I told you exactly who they'd have her killed."

"So why tell me now?" Mackenzie asked, feeling the room spin slightly as she reeled.

"Well clearly they've given you this information to try and leverage you also. Me telling you this now changes nothing. I'm sorry I didn't, but she's my best friend and there's no way either of us can help her. I wish we could, but they are just too powerful," Vicki explained.

It was as though Mackenzie had downed half a bottle of tequila. At Vicki's words, the world seemed to tip violently, a dizziness settling over her as she absorbed the words she heard. Horror and anger at this woman who'd joined her life flared inside her, boiling her organs as she thought over the cowardice. "So what? We just let her rot wherever they have her hidden away?" Mackenzie couldn't help the volume her voice reached as she tried to hold back her own true emotions, feeling the guilt inside Vicki rise to the surface.

Mackenzie didn't care.

"We just need to adhere to their requests and maybe we can barter a deal for her release in return for something they want," Vicki said, trying to be diplomatic but it did nothing to soften her initial words.

It occurred to Mackenzie that despite what Vicki had withheld, her neighbor really didn't know the true powers or intents of this organization. They wouldn't release her mother, and if they did, it would be at the sacrifice of Mackenzie's family power and her newly acquired one. She couldn't give that up; it was something she couldn't have imagined her father would have wanted to do or else he would've in his time. Surely.

"And if they don't? She's been locked away for ten years, who's to say she wouldn't be locked away for another ten if we do nothing?" Mackenzie yelled at Vicki.

"Surely there's something they want enough to trade her for?"

"Maybe… but what if it's wanting me dead? Or what if they know when they hand her over they don't have control over us anymore? This is a secret organization that has the only leverage against us to stop us from telling anyone or acting against them. Do you really think they will ever give that up?"

Mackenzie watched as the reality of what she was saying dawned on her mother's best friend. As though in ten years she had never considered this information – or hadn't wanted to.

"There's got to be something," Vicki reiterated, her voice breaking, and Mackenzie could see her for exactly what she was: a woman scared for her friend but too afraid to act against the organization. Vicki was right; she had no magic and no way of acting against them.

But Mackenzie did.

"There isn't. Unless you've heard otherwise, I'm not going to stop looking for her or trying to get her back," Mackenzie said defiantly, sitting up straight on the edge of the couch as she met Vicki's gaze unflinchingly. Mackenzie didn't care what it took, how long, or how much of herself she had to use to fight against them, she would do it. She'd save her mother because after ten years convinced her mother was dead, she had to.

"I'm begging you not to. They won't like it," Vicki said, the fear in her voice and emotions made Mackenzie's skin crawl. The inflections in her tone had the hairs on her arms standing up as though at any moment something sinister would jump out of a hiding place to come and kill both of them. There was a tremble in her voice that only made Mackenzie want to console her more – to be more sure of her eventual victory over the Arcana.

"They don't have to. But I'm getting her back."

"I love your mother like she was my own sister, but they'll hurt her if you don't stop."

"They might hurt her if I do."

"They won't. I know they won't," Vicki said, her voice shaking even more.

Something about it made Mackenzie stand up

quickly, her own limbs shaking. "You can't know that."

"They told me she'll be hurt if you don't stop." Vicki's voice broke and everything in Mackenzie went cold at the realization. That icy darkness in her threatened to take on the world with her anger.

"Who told you about my accident?" Mackenzie said bluntly, poison in her tone.

"Mackenzie, please. I – "

"*Who?*" she interrupted, the sharp edge threatening to slice anyone who came too close as any empathy for Vicki disappeared.

"The Arcana did. They told me that if you didn't stop looking for your mother and asking questions, they would ensure there was no one to find," Vicki admitted quietly, dropping her eye contact as Mackenzie held back the part of her that wanted to fling items around the room with her powers like a magical toddler throwing a tantrum.

Hot, angry tears welled in her eyes as she watched Vicki sag in shame, feeling the rancid taste of it in her emotional aura.

"How do you know they aren't already hurting her? Who's to say they haven't already killed her and just telling you she's fine?" she bit at Vicki, watching as nothing in her expression fought that notion.

Vicki had no idea if her mother was really alive, and there was no guarantee the Arcana wasn't lying to them and just leveraging them without providing proof of life and wellness.

Vicki stayed silent.

"I *will not* negotiate with a corrupt organization that can't even prove they have my mother and she's alive and well. For all you know, they've been lying to you and my mother disappeared years ago and stayed out of their reach," Mackenzie stated, waiting for any words to spill from Vicki – either in regret or clarification. None came. "Never ask that of me again."

Vicki's bottom lip shook as she looked up at

Mackenzie from her seat on the couch, blinking through the forming tears. "Please, Mackenzie, I beg of you. Don't give them reason to hurt her."

"I won't let her live her life in torture. If she even is alive," Mackenzie said, surprised at her own revelations. Parts of her hardened as she fought her own fears of the fate of her mother. "Now get the fuck out of my house."

"Mackenzie –"

"Get *the fuck* out."

For a breath, Vicki hesitated and Mackenzie considered what she could conjure to move her out of the house quickly.

Before she had to, Vicki lifted herself off the couch, the tears finally falling, and walked back towards the front door.

Despite the overwhelming fear and worry that had once again overtaken her mother's best friend, Mackenzie couldn't find it in her to care about Vicki's emotions.

Vicki halted at the door, her hand on the handle as she looked back at Mackenzie, who stayed rooted to the spot in the living area, avoiding doing something with her magic in her anger that she might regret.

"I hope you know what you're doing," Vicki said just loud enough for Mackenzie to hear the words as they shook in her throat.

"All I can say, Vicki, is if it was my best friend taken by them, magic or not, I would be fighting with everything I had *every single day* to rescue her."

Mackenzie barely heard the slam of the front door over the blood pumping through her ears.

8: THE WANDS RETURN

Mackenzie was covered in sweat… again. It seemed like this would be a new state of being she would have to embrace as she fought not to lose her posture in the cold, echoey martial arts gym. Sucking in gulps of air through her teeth, Mackenzie tried not to smell the pungent odor of sweat that permeated the space. And yet, despite her best attempts to only breathe in through her mouth, it still turned her nose up in disgust.

With a final tight bow, Grant called that the class was dismissed in the serious martial-arts tone she hadn't heard before in his HIIT workouts. It was a reverent kind of serious he brought on when he was taking a martial arts class, as opposed to his friendly drill-sergeant he brought out for her usual workout classes. It was an interesting and refreshing change.

As Mackenzie's body relaxed to the 'at ease' command, she shivered in tiredness - the sort she hadn't felt before, the kind that came from holding your body stiffly in brand new postures it wasn't used to. While the multi-level class had walked through actions and maneuvers with the higher belts she could only hope to achieve one day, her exercises ranged from learning how to kick and punch in a way they hadn't taught her in the boxing HIIT class. Doing it with Grant in his workout class had in no way prepared her for what she'd experience here, and the length of time she had to hold her new 'stances' for was continual, not in intervals like she'd hoped.

But despite the soreness and sheer exhaustion in her body, it felt *good*. She knew her body was slowly tearing her muscles up only to return stronger and more prepared the next time. She was thankful for the invite to the class, and happy with her decision to come.

Mackenzie reminded herself to thank Kai for pushing her to attend when she returned home. Catching Grant's eye as he farewelled others with a soft smile, she watched as he excused himself from chatting with one of the other black belts and walked over to her slowly, giving her a chance to escape this time if she chose to.

"Hey, Mac. Glad you could join us. How did you enjoy your first Taekwondo class?" he asked, crossing his arms and leaning his upper torso back in a relaxed way, like doing all the maneuvers with his students had done nothing to tire his fitness level, and showed off exactly why he was the owner and founder of the gym. His forearms bulged slightly at the motion.

"It was good. I really had no idea what to expect and I'm sure my muscles will hate me later for it, but it's a start towards where I want to be. Feeling more powerful and able to protect myself physically is definitely the goal," she replied, feeling the way her insides warmed comfortingly as she ran a hand over her sweat-slicked hair, smoothing out any fly-away strands from her ringleted mess of a ponytail. *At least physically stronger when magic isn't involved,* she reminded herself. There was still a whole area of ability she needed to master in order to ensure those with magic couldn't overpower her, because they were the ones likely to be after her.

"It's a good martial art for distance, that's for sure," he agreed, nodding, but the word choice stuck out, pulling Mackenzie's lips into a confused frown.

"Distance?"

"Well, learning how to kick, punch and block. All very helpful skills in a fistfight but not in a close quarters fight, or if you get taken to the ground," Grant said, conjuring the memory in Mackenzie's mind of Teo on top of her as they fought months ago, and how helpless she had felt physically, only her magic and the bracelets able to save her.

That needed to change.

"And which martial art helps with that?"

"One of the wrestling-style martial arts, like wrestling obviously, Brazilian Jiu Jitsu, or Judo. Sometimes even Hapkido."

Mackenzie stared blankly, feeling him lose her as the list continued, each more foreign to her than the last. "I'm pretty sure you're just making up words now." She laughed, feeling so out of her depth as she wondered how many styles of martial arts even existed. Her knowledge of the world felt so limited and small compared to the world of learning she hadn't yet even brushed. It thrilled her and stirred her defiance and body into readiness for whatever the world threw at her. It seemed every interaction she had with Grant made her feel powerful and excited to experience a new strength she hadn't found before.

"Not at all." He chuckled along with her, his voice soft as he explained. "Different languages. I know it can seem like a lot but they are all definitely real. You can stay for the next hour and see what you think of BJJ, if you want?"

"Why not!" she agreed, watching his face light up in response as she turned her back on her gym bag, ready to face whatever came next.

"That's the spirit! Here's one of my main guys arriving now. He helps me take the class occasionally," Grant said, flourishing his hand towards the door that had opened, a burst of ice wind following the newcomer in.

Mackenzie turned and caught sight of chestnut brown hair, tan skin and dark eyes. Her shaking muscles stiffened, readying once again for a fight as she recognized the tall, muscled man before her.

Nothing had changed in him since the night she'd last seen him at the frat house party, besides his clean shaven face now peppered with stubble making him seem older... more rugged... more dangerous. The name escaped her, but the sight of him shot fear through her bloodstream.

"Mackenzie, meet Matt," Grant said as the man walked over.

It was clear the moment he'd caught sight of her by the quick tightening of his angular jawline and visible slow swallow as he fought the frown crowding his face. He recovered quickly though, looking at Grant and letting his face lighten in response. "We've actually met before!" he said with a nod and a tight smile, glancing at Mackenzie again as she fought not to run.

She wasn't sure how to react, whether she should play it cool in front of Grant or disappear and never return to martial arts classes – despite her new love of them. She chose the former, letting Matt decide the way this played out.

"Oh?"

"Your new initiate here actually came to the frat's big bash a few months ago! She did leave before we could properly get... acquainted," Matt drawled, his expression guarded in a way that could be interpreted as sexual or flirty by those without the knowledge, but Mackenzie could tell it was intended as a warning that he knew *exactly* who she was.

Mackenzie pushed her magical awareness out, brushing out against his emotions warily. Hot anger nearly burned her, making her recoil, hoping it wouldn't push on her.

Grant's side-eye to Mackenzie as she tried to keep her face as innocent and free from fear as possible told her that he believed Matt to be interested in her. He stepped back slightly, with a small smile, catching the gaze of another newcomer to the class with a nod. "I'll... leave you to it for a moment and just check with Paul that he's okay to help demonstrate today. Matt, can I leave you in charge of our new white belt?"

"No problem, Grant." He answered before Mackenzie could open her mouth and ask Grant not to leave her alone with his other instructor.

Grant disappeared with barely a nod and Mackenzie couldn't help the way her heart smashed into her ribs as she turned to Matt, wide-eyed and fearful of what he would do to her. *Could* he do anything in such a public place, or were they all in on it? What if everyone in this gym was an Order of Wands member, out to get her if they knew who she was?

"Well, if it isn't the newest *Arcana* initiate," he said quietly enough that only the two of them could hear, a growl in the back of his throat.

"You must be late to your intel. I'm no Arcana initiate," she whispered, her eyes dropping to the floor as the blood pumped through her ears. She hoped it would halt him from doing anything – setting the record straight – but she couldn't be sure if it would, given that she'd stolen the artifact they could have been protecting for generations.

"Oh? And why's that?" he asked a little louder, drawing her frightened gaze. She struggled to keep her gaze steady with his, glancing around to check whether they were being overheard in the gym, despite its relative emptiness.

She still didn't know how safe she was in this place anymore.

Matt watched her though, the anger seeming to have loosened from his features as he crossed his arms across his chest and leaned his upper body away, surveying her head to toe in the quiet.

"Look, I know you probably don't like me," she said in a hushed voice as she leaned forward, pleading with his curiosity rather than his anger, hoping she could diffuse it all. "But trust me when I say I'm not with the

Arcana."

With relief, she could see it remove more and more anger as she spoke but now she just had to figure out how much information she could divulge.

"I'll admit, it's a little bit confusing that you stole the one item the Major Arcana has wanted in their possession since we became its protectors, *and yet* the person who came to protect you when we caught up to you was none other than the Devil wielder himself, Kai Logan."

His use of Kai's full name made her mouth flail for a moment and his familiarity with the syllables made her brow furrow as she waited for the question that seemed to be coming. None came.

"You know Kai?"

"I know he's no friend of the Arcana's. And he's no enemy of ours but, for you, he was throwing me around like a dog's chew toy."

At the memory of Kai in his beast form, tossing Matt's body from between his teeth off into the distance to protect her, her cheeks flushed. She didn't know why she was embarrassed that her now-boyfriend had been around to protect her, but maybe that he had fought those he had considered allies for her. It definitely made her warm at the thought, wishing Kai were there to embrace.

As her gaze returned to the moment at hand, she realized Matt was waiting for her to respond. "I... was in a confused place back then, but all you need to know is the bracelets never ended up with the Arcana. I might have wanted an in with them once, but I've seen the error of my ways," she said, seeing his surprised half-grin as though he were almost impressed at her revelations.

"Well, that's... good. Want to return the bracelets to us then? We have the ability to keep them safe from the Arcana." His arms were still crossed but his body had relaxed and he looked at Mackenzie almost... playfully as he spoke softly.

"Why? Because you're a group of big strong men and I'm just a poor little Magician who can't protect what she managed to take from you?" She grinned, watching his eyes narrow as he assessed her comments.

She couldn't gauge much about him but he didn't stiffen or anger at her comment; no flux of irritation from his aura touched her, only curiosity and ease. She became hyper-aware of how horrid she must look, coated in sweat from the class before, wearing a stiff new taekwondo uniform she wasn't sure she looked comfortable in yet. It certainly wasn't well-fitted or flattering when she'd seen it in the mirror earlier, and yet he looked her up and down like he could see through it all – not in a leering way, but rather assessing the barter opponent in front of him.

"No. It's what the Order of Wands was created for."

"Huh?"

"Surely you've read the book of your ancestors…"

"I mean, it specified back with Sarah Good's daughter, the first Magician, that the Order of Wands was created but it never detailed what for, and that's assuming you've kept the same mission since then."

"The Orders – all of them – were created when the powers were split into family lines to serve the strongest members of the tarot. The Order of Wands – unsurprisingly – for the Magician. And as your line split from the mission of the Arcana, so did we."

The words hit her like a physical flick to the forehead, her mouth dropping open and flapping about like a fish as she thought over what he was saying. She couldn't help the grin at the sheer ridiculousness of the notion – one that no one had thought to mention to her since she'd been awakened. "I have a whole house of men who are supposed to serve me?" She held in the laugh that wanted to bubble up her throat.

"Don't make it sound like some weird reverse harem!" he guffawed.

Mackenzie's eyes bulged and everything in her face flushed with heat hotter than when she'd been exercising through martial arts. She knew she was bright red as the shock registered. "I wasn't… I didn't… That's not…" she stumbled, interrupted by Grant yelling out to the room.

Mackenzie was suddenly aware of how full the gym was of people – large muscled men and a few well-toned women – in uniforms slightly different from hers, ready to start.

"Everyone on the mats," Grant called, barely giving Mackenzie and Matt a second look as his eyes swept the room.

Mackenzie turned back to Matt quickly, determined to set the record straight, to catch him watching her with a knowing grin on his face.

Before she could speak contrary to his belief, he tapped her on the back of the shoulder and headed to line up with the others. "We'll talk after this, MacDaddy. Let's roll first."

"Roll?" she echoed, following him on to the mats with a confusion that said she wasn't necessary going to like the answer.

The next hour was an experience Mackenzie was not mentally prepared for. Matt was in charge of teaching her the basics of Brazilian Jiu Jitsu while the rest of the class worked on exercises and maneuvers they were all well-versed in – very similar to Taekwondo. What she discovered not long after beginning the class was that when Grant had mentioned close-quarters combat and rolling, he had meant it whole-heartedly.

Mackenzie drilled with Matt ways to overpower an opponent when they had her pinned in various ways, the entire time so hyper-aware of where each of their limbs pressed against each other's, how close his body was to hers, and how nights before Kai had used these sorts of moves to have his way with her.

Not once did she ever sense arousal from Matt, ever

the professional as he spoke about ways to protect her safety while being in such closeness.

Her already-exhausted muscles were so tired that any resistance seemed to strain her body until it didn't want to comply. She continued to fight though, attempting to do a maneuver and move or roll him off in different ways. Either his fight was stronger than 'going easy on her' like he complained, or she desperately needed to improve her strength abilities – and quickly.

It was abysmal regardless and all she wanted in that moment was months more training to not look as weak as she felt against the Order of Wands member teaching her sparring.

9: THE NEW TEAM

The early twilight air felt less cold with Matt by Mackenzie's side. The light danced in interesting ways through the sky, like it was speaking only to her as it played with the horizon. Power, despite the exhaustion, coursed through her veins and for the first time wandering around in Salem, she felt truly safe from the Arcana.

Maybe it was the sheer size of Matt, the way he had demonstrated takedowns on other members of the class halfway through the hour, but she felt confident that the Arcana would and could do nothing with him walking her home.

He'd offered, and she had seen it as the perfect opportunity for him to meet the rest of her chosen family, likely sitting at home on the couch considering dinner. Pulling out her phone quickly as they wandered through the main street, she sped through a text to her group chat with Kai and Lucy.

MACKENZIE: PLEASE TELL ME YOU TWO ARE AT HOME.
LUCY: YES, WHY'S THAT?
MACKENZIE: I HAVE ACQUIRED A NEW MEMBER FOR OUR ANTI-ARCANA TEAM.
LUCY: OH?
MACKENZIE: YOU'LL SEE.
KAI: WHO?
MACKENZIE: ARE YOU AT HOME?

KAI: YES.
MACKENZIE: THEN YOU'LL SEE SHORTLY. BRINGING
HIM BACK FOR A DEBRIEF AWAY FROM ARCANA EARS.
LUCY: OKAY. SEE YOU SOON.

Mackenzie couldn't help feeling rejected as Kai read the message, seemed to type a reply and then didn't respond. Unease snuck into her utter confidence, threatening to break her down. Shaking the thought away, convinced she was just overthinking, she slid her phone back into her pocket and looked at Matt with a smile, determined not to be rude and show him her full attention.

"Sorry about that, they'll be ready for us at home," she said quickly, feeling breathless as the cold air dried her throat near instantly. Somehow, though, the cold had barely reached her body, and not only because of the oversized hoodie of Kai's she had conveniently borrowed – she was on top of the world. As much as she could be when she still had problems to solve and muscles to massage.

"Great! You know, you did well today for a beginner. We'll have you pro in no time." He grinned back at her, making her feel warm at the praise, her energy renewed by his validation.

"Thanks! I tried. It was really a bit unnerving to begin with…"

"How so?"

"Well, think of how daunting it is practicing how to defend against a man on top of you." She watched understanding straighten the frowning concern on his face as he followed her train of thought, nodding. "I understand the usefulness – believe me, *I know* – but it's a confronting thing to practice nonetheless."

"You know?" he asked, his face once again scrunching up as he considered her words. There was no judgement in his features, only concern.

She opened her mouth, considering how much she

should tell him for a moment, but let the powerful drive inside her embolden her to tell her story. "Right after I got the bracelets, the Arcana tried to blackmail me into giving them up. It turned into a skirmish that ended with Teo physically and magically overpowering me until the bracelets became active and I took his power. If I hadn't taken his power away and gotten lucky with a couple of hits, I don't know where I'd be right now."

"I'm sorry to hear that!" Matt said softly. "If you need to practice, in future, with a woman to make it easier, that can be arranged."

"Oh no!" Mackenzie reeled, horrified at the insinuation she'd given him, backpedaling through her own words as she floundered for how rescind her insult. "Nothing is wrong with your teaching! I was just trying to point out how new of a concept it was for me and that it was a lot for me to wrap my head around. You are fine. It was just an entirely different vibe from Taekwondo."

The side street she often detoured into appeared beside her and she led the way off the main street, enjoying the quieting of less people and the freedom to speak more openly.

"I'll bet!" Matt said, thankful for the lighter topic. "Admittedly BJJ is a lot more practically helpful in a fight and if you're going to be taking on the Arcana, you're going to need every bit of help you can get."

She smiled softly as she met his warm dark brown eyes. "I appreciate the help from the Order of Wands too. Hopefully it can sway the power dynamic in our favor – but we can talk more on that where we're less likely to be heard."

Despite the near-empty, cold street around them, Mackenzie could still feel the twinge at the back of her neck that said she was being watched. She didn't know if it was paranoia or reality, but she figured she would trust it for the moment, at least until she was in the safety of her own home.

Matt nodded his agreement as he too glanced around, his emotional aura flashing with a wariness that pricked her like a needle she hadn't realized she'd touched.

They made it to the edge of the Common, Matt checking the space around them as recognition tightened his eyes. He clearly knew where they were but was questioning how close they were to her home.

Warily, Mackenzie stepped onto the grass, feeling the presence of the gazebo like a weight that refused to leave her shoulders. Matt, clearly, didn't know what she was so tense around, his body radiating the same calm security in his stance and aura as it had when they'd left. He clocked her continuous glances at the structure in the middle of the Salem Common but held no recognition as he looked at what must have been a normal fixture in his life, living next to it. How he'd never noticed the magic presences around it or the entry and exit, she didn't know.

When they finally arrived in front of Mackenzie's house, she stopped, letting the location of where they were sink in. She knew the moment it did by the way he curled over his knees and let out a heavy sigh and a breathy laugh of disbelief.

"No… way!" Matt said, returning himself to an upright position as he watched the house wide-eyed, running a hand through his already-tousled hair.

"What?"

"You've been telling me, this whole time, the bracelets have been this close to the frat house and we had no idea? You were under our noses the entire time!" He sighed, yet no anger or frustration reached her from his emotional aura as she sought it out, feeling only the light weightlessness of disbelief and a slight tingle of… amusement?

"Yes…" Her cheeks flushed as she led the way into the house so they could talk more freely. Pulling her key out and unlocking the door quickly, she peeked her head around the wood of the door to find Lucy and Kai already seated in the living area off the main hall. Before she heralded the way, she caught the glimpse of the serious expressions as they turned to her entry.

"Am I interrupting?" she asked, sure she was but not sure they would continue it with her in the room.

Kai looked as though he might, his face tightening as he glanced at Lucy before he tried to answer, but Mackenzie's blonde bombshell of a best friend opened her mouth and cut him off before he could try speaking. "Not at all! Let's meet the newest member of the team!"

Mackenzie moved further in, leaving space for Matt to follow her inside before she shut the door behind him and indicated the way to the living area. "Lucy, this is Matt. Kai, you'd already know our new friend from the Order of Wands," she said with a smile and a flourish at the tall man standing beside her, becoming very aware that they were both messed from their sweat-induced session that – despite the perspiration now well and truly gone – had left them in a state of disarray. Glancing at Kai, it was clear as he looked between them he was noticing it too and by the sheer wall of uncomfortable irritation growing in him, he was assuming many things by this.

"The Order of Wands? As in the people we robbed a few months ago?" Lucy blurted, uncaring of how it sounded to all ears.

Trying to hide a grin, Mackenzie nodded, seeing the way Lucy's eyes widened as she assessed more of Matt's figure through the thin gym clothing on his bulky, muscled frame.

"The very same. But as I explained to Matt, that was when I was trying to get inside the Major Arcana's operation and before I discovered the true extent of their motives. I know better now." Despite feeling no animosity from Matt, she wanted him to be sure he could trust her and that there was no doubt in his mind about her disloyalty towards the Major Arcana.

"So how did you two meet?" Lucy pushed, with a telling grin to Mackenzie. Mackenzie recognized the expression, similar to the one Lucy had worn the day they'd first come in contact with Kai. The look that said a mischievous potential adventure idea was running through her best friend's mind.

The frown Mackenzie returned to her best friend told her everything she needed to know: *Definitely not even a thought. Stop it.* "I ran into Matt at my martial arts class," she said simply, returning her tone to the lighter, simple one she used that was difficult to interpret any other way than kind.

The weird angst building in Kai wasn't quelled by the nice, platonic tone – if anything, at her words, she felt the horrible rancid taste of jealousy in her mouth that she was sure was originating from him.

"How convenient," Lucy replied, ignoring the ball of foul emotion that was Kai beside her as her tone flirted with normal conversation.

Mackenzie wished she could beg Lucy telepathically to stop but alas, that was not in her power.

"It's good to see you, man," Matt said, stepping forward to Kai for a half-hug, half pat on the back of which Kai returned, albeit stiffly.

'You too," Kai muttered tightly as he pulled back from the brotherly embrace.

When Matt stood back, he turned back to Mackenzie expectantly, a ready soft smile pulling at his lips. "Okay, so now we're in a safe area away from the Arcana possibly overhearing, what do you need help with that the Order of Wands can assist with?"

Mackenzie was aback with how ready he was to help her. "Wow, you guys really are serious about serving the Magicians bloodline."

"It is our job and we haven't been able to do it for a while. So let's hear it…"

"I want to go up against the Arcana. The first thing for me to deal with though is they took my mother a number of years ago, but I've only just discovered that she's still alive. She's been missing – presumed dead – for ten years, and I need to save her. Any assistance from the Order of the Wands in finding and retrieving her from wherever she is would be greatly appreciated."

Silence fell for a moment until Matt nodded, taking in all the information and weighing up if it was something the Order could help with.

A wave of jealousy came off Kai as Mackenzie lit up at the acceptance.

"We can help with that. We've been keeping tabs and spying on the Arcana as best we can in the absence of a Magician."

"Do you have much intel to share?"

"Not as much as we'd ideally like, but probably more than you've been able to get. They're very wary of you from what we could tell recently; I imagine it's been since you moved to town. Thankfully, they've forgotten about us for the most part, except as holders of the artifact you stole. They likely assumed we were lost without the next Magician to guide us." A hint of a wicked grin lingered in his smile, making her return his amusement.

"Well, weren't you?" she joked, flipping her hair back in mock vanity, hearing Lucy join in as she giggled away.

Kai seethed with a flare of jealousy that almost physically struck her.

Uncaring of the rest of the room, feeling his negative emotions like a wound, she lost her amusement and looked up at him through raised, annoyed eyebrows. "What?" she said flatly.

His eyes widened as he searched for the words to say that didn't make him sound like a petty dick. "Nothing… Just not sure how they are going to help us find your mother when we've been searching for months," he said, but clearly he didn't realize the sheer volume of his emotions, broadcasting his every feeling to her.

"And how were we going to find her on our own when we've been doing exactly that with no return?"

Silence fell between them, her eyes glaring holes into his pupils as she imagined what it would be like to have laser heat vision in that moment.

His emotions bashed into her in growing waves, anger bursting to join his initial jealousy.

"I'm not here to step on any one's toes. I'm only here to help," Matt said diplomatically, his hands slightly bending back at the wrists, looking between Kai and Mackenzie, apparently ready to jump in to break up any physical altercation.

"Well, I guess we'll see how helpful you guys can be," Kai said tightly, but the war inside still threatened to scar Mackenzie with its pointedness.

She broke his gaze, returning to see Matt watching them carefully. Smiling and trying to break the tension, her shoulders relaxed as she breathed deeply. Taking note of the strain in Matt's smile, guilt punched her in the gut at the thought of what she'd brought him into, even though all she wanted to do was yell at Kai for the way he'd made him feel. With a dangerous quick glance at Kai, dropping the smile, she returned in full energy to the conversation with Matt. "I'm really sorry. It doesn't seem like a great time, but I'm so grateful for any help the Order of Wands are willing to provide. For intel on my mother or even just possible places to search for more information…" She gave a hopeful smile that Matt was more than willing to reciprocate as they forgot about Kai's discomfort for a moment.

"No problem, Big Mac. I'll be in touch," he responded, fishing his phone from his pocket, thumbing to the contacts and handing it to her.

She took it without hesitation, the boil of anger in Kai growing as her hand touched the device but she fought through it, ignoring the loud emotion in her mind she couldn't ignore.

"I'll let you know when I have something to share from the Order."

With a nod, Mackenzie walked behind Matt to the front door, showing him out slowly. The warm power she'd felt before was gradually being replaced by an absolute fury at Kai's rudeness and utter pigheadedness in the face of someone who could only bring them good fortune in their fight against the Arcana.

Stomping back to the living area, she saw Lucy picking at her nails, relatively oblivious to the chaos that was about to unfold as she opened her mouth to unload her own emotions on Kai. It was only fair.

"Care to explain what that was?"

Lucy's head snapped up from her cuticles at the sound of Mackenzie's tone: flat, sharp and pointed at Kai as his eyebrows shot towards his forehead, feigning innocence as he bullshitted his answers.

"I think you're too trusting of someone who had you pinned to a tree a few months ago as his enemy."

"Because I snuck into their house and stole one of the main things of the Magician's they were sworn to protect from the Arcana."

"I just think we need to be cautious…"

"Is it *us* who needs to be cautious… or me?"

"What do you mean?"

"You don't think I can't feel the jealousy rolling off you in painful waves?"

The silence in the room descended harshly and was something she could tell Lucy was choosing not to wade through. Lucy's full lips tightened into a thin line as she quietly waved her goodbye and ducked off to the kitchen.

Both Kai and Mackenzie followed her disappearance for barely a moment before returning to each other's tense glares. The guilt that had leaked into his emotional aura was palpable, a heavy weight pushing against his jealousy, but not quite winning, encouraging Mackenzie that she was on the right track.

"You randomly come home from martial arts with a new guy in tow and are suddenly all trusting of him, how am I supposed to feel? I know he teaches jiu jitsu, I've taken his classes, so you've probably been rolling around with him for the last hour, if not two," Kai said

Mackenzie's jaw dropped open like it had lost the muscle power to stay shut. She wouldn't have been surprised if a click had opened it to indicate it had officially lost all power to hold itself at all. Only the pure flash of hurt sent the words hurling from her before she could stop them, loud and vocal – even Lucy would be able to hear them wherever she'd disappeared to. "You're supposed to trust your girlfriend!"

"I do trust you," he whispered, as though he could stop her outburst by lowering his own. He seemed to think that if he quieted, she would match him – but he had lit a fire in her stomach that needed to be breathed out in her anger and all he could do was withstand it.

"Do you? You don't think if he was turned on rolling around with me that I'd be able to sense it? That I wouldn't excuse myself from the situation? Do you think so little of me?"

She could see the way her words settled over him, pulling his features down, making him realize how his opinions and lack of trust had made him look – what he thought of her. He opened his mouth and closed it a few times, finally considering what to say as the jealousy in him subsided more and more. She could see the racing thoughts behind his eyes as his mind ran over what he was voicing, watching him settle on something.

She watched, her mouth now holding itself together in a tense line that she was sure was nearly straight in shape. Finally, after a few moments waiting for him to decide, she resigned to believe he would insult her yet again.

Kai breathed defeatedly, sighing as his gaze dropped to the ground."I'm sorry. I wasn't thinking straight. I know Matt well, we grew up together and… he was always good at getting the girl, I just assumed he'd put the moves on you," Kai admitted, his cheeks turning pink like a little boy who'd been caught doing something he shouldn't have.

The sheer sight of his guilty embarrassment and the fact he'd been willing to admit it quelled the angry beast rising inside Mackenzie. A heavy breath escaped her too, released the tension that had been building inside her already exhausted muscles, leaving them shaky and ready for a shower to mend them.

She moved forward, closer to Kai, feeling her insides soften as she approached him. "Even if he had – which he didn't – I can take care of myself. Especially now that I have these emotion powers. People can't hide their feelings from me, including you. I can sense when you're getting jealous and not letting me look after it. We aren't going to work if you don't trust me. No more jealous douche act, okay?"

He nodded slowly, moving his bicep into her touch as she reached for his arm where it hung relaxed beside him. He raised it, sliding it around her waist as he pulled her closer inch by inch.

She leaned back to keep an eye on his face, making sure he understood how serious she was on the topic despite her softened anger.

"You're right. I guess… the world has been in so much chaos that we haven't really been able to focus on forming the relationship right. I was a prick, I'm sorry," he said through gritted teeth as his guilt washed over them again.

"You're going to have to straighten your shit out with Matt too, eventually, if we're all going to work together. Make sure you two are okay?"

"I will."

"Good. And please, Kai, trust me."

"I do. I'm sorry. You do know what you're doing and I need to back that in everything: men, life, decisions about the Arcana. I need to be your support, not the person who questions it. It's a work in progress – just *trust me* when I tell you, I'm working on it."

She searched his eyes, seeing the truth in them as his fingers traced her lower back, both his arms now up and circling her waist. "I appreciate being defended and protected to a *point*. But there are limits."

'I'll keep myself and the beast in check," He nodded in agreement as he pulled her into a hug.

Surrendering to the warmth, she hugged him back, feeling his muscles ripple as she too played with the tip of her nails along his spine in return. His breath was heavy as his body rumbled under her touch and as she leaned backwards out of the hug, she found her head tipped back, exposing her neck as his lips lightly scraped along her skin.

Every nerve in her buzzed and she could already feel the way the heat rushed between her legs as one of his hands slid down over her butt cheek, cupping with his fingers dangerously close to the gathering warmth. She sucked in air, nearly moaning as his tongue traced the vein on the side of her neck that pumped the blood to her head, the motion making her crave more.

His face moving up slightly, his teeth scraping her earlobe, her hips pressed forward as she leaned further back into his strong, tight arms, feeling the way the bulge in the front of his pants seemed to stir at her pelvis' nearby presence.

His face reached hers, kissed her slowly, making her taste every single moment of their connection until all she longed for was to feel his tongue taste every bit of her…

She pulled herself up straight, kissing him once more before disconnecting from the touch with a grin. "Nope, I'm not rewarding bad behavior." She chuckled. "You get none of that from me right now. We just drove Lucy out of the room, I want to see what she thinks of this, you can cool off and maybe later, if you're lucky, I'll let you at some of this."

Stepping back, Mackenzie headed for the main entry hall, feeling Kai's presence right behind her, a reminder of what she was avoiding.

"If you say so," he said with a rasp in his throat that had parts of her melting at the sound. She knew that voice was reserved just for when she'd driven him wild. "I might go for a walk to get rid of this extra… energy… and see if I can catch up with Matt to apologize now."

"Good boy." She giggled as she moved to open the front door for him.

His hand slid up the inside of her thigh until a soft cry escaped her lips as he found wetness she had wanted to hide from him. She didn't want to admit how quickly he could turn her on, especially when an argument was involved.

"Careful," he whispered in her ear, his breath tickling the hairs on her cheek. "Keep praising me and I might just make sure you scream that out for everyone to hear."

Before she could gulp in the lost breath, Kai had disappeared out the front door, leaving her flushed and wet, unsure how to proceed.

10: THE FOOL'S EQUATION

For a moment, the front door seemed like a foreign object to her brain that was entirely consumed by the image of Kai having his way with her – any way with her, she could imagine many different scenarios for what he would do to her. And yet, it took her minutes to register that he had in fact left and she needed to return to reality and not linger in the daydream of him.

With a deep breath, Mackenzie followed her nose – the smell of ham and cheese melts wafting from the kitchen as Lucy made yet another meal in lieu of listening to Kai and Mackenzie's tough conversations.

Leaning on the doorframe of the kitchen walkway, Mackenzie watched as Lucy painstakingly measured the halfway marker on her sandwich and cut perfectly center, the way she always liked to. The eccentricities of her best friend sometimes made Mackenzie smile, and she found herself quite content just to watch Lucy work away on her food, hyper-focused on the task at hand.

"I'm going to assume by your presence in the kitchen that you two have worked your problems out?" Lucy said, her eyes never leaving the toasted bread in front of her as she finally had it cut perfectly, lifting it from the plate and stuffing it between her teeth. Only then did she turn to meet her friend's gaze, content.

"Good guess. He was just being a bit of an idiot and needs to learn how to trust me," Mackenzie said lightheartedly, as though it hadn't just torn her up inside and made her angrier than she thought possible.

She could feel the hints of doubt in Lucy now but they both knew she could sense it. They'd never needed magic powers to understand each other however.

"You two haven't really had the quiet time to yourselves to learn that, though. Since you two met the world has always been ending or there's something more important than building that intimacy. I'd go easy on him, at least a little. Plus, it wasn't as bad as you're making it out to be with Matt, you probably just noticed it more because of the emotion-reading thing."

"You think?"

"Well, if you hadn't jumped on Kai about it, Matt probably wouldn't have figured any of that out. He might have just assumed Kai was being wary of trusting a new person in the fold. You were the one that let the jealous cat out of the bag and made it clear what was happening…" Lucy explained, not holding back.

Mackenzie's face burned as her cheeks flushed and she began chewing on her lip. "I… didn't know it wasn't obvious."

"I get it, but I'm just saying be aware of yourself. You notice so much more than you used to now because of the new powers you've unleashed. You feel all the nuances we miss because you feel it so wholeheartedly. Like everything, there's a pro and a con, it's just about awareness of the con so you can minimize its damage on the people you love."

"When did you become so wise?"

"Always have been. I just keep my nuggets of wisdom to myself most of the time. Can't let you have all the fun."

Mackenzie opened her mouth, nearly to tell her that it wasn't 'fun', but shut it quickly as she assessed her best friend. The half-smirk on her face was one that had always been there to help cheer Mackenzie up with the quick quips when she needed it, and Mackenzie couldn't help the burst of warmth she felt for her best friend.

"Thank you, Luce," she said quietly, bursting forward and wrapping her arms around Lucy's upper body, squeezing tightly and not loosening until she felt her best friend return the gesture. She reveled in the feeling for a moment, the warmth and perfect fit, sating something deep in her soul.

"Always, KZ," Lucy said, finally moving out of the hug and beaming with a mixture of pride and playfulness. "Speaking of pros and cons, having Matt on our team is *definitely* a pro."

"Having the Order of Wands on our side is a great new development for team Magician."

"No, I mean 'cause he's so yummy!"

"Lucy!" Mackenzie gaped, grabbing the dishtowel from the top of the bench and whipping it at her friend with a disbelieving laugh.

"What? A girl can look!"

"You can do more than look if you want to. You're gorgeous, sweet, and amazing, he couldn't do much better than you… That is, if you wanted to ask him out?"

"Aww, thanks KZ. Look who's pushing me to be social now? Good job! I appreciate it, but I may already have my sights on someone already."

"What?! Why didn't you tell me this sooner?" Mackenzie cried excitedly, feeling like the two of them had returned to old times all over again and the world was normal. "Who, what, when, where, why? I need all the details. Now, please," For a moment they could almost pretend that nothing was threatening them outside the house and no one was missing.

Mackenzie wished it could be their own little world just for one small moment in time before she had to return to the real world of magic, arcane societies, and chaos.

"His name is Tyler and I met him at work."

"Oh come on, more details than that. Do you work

with him?"

"No, he was a customer but he comes in all the time now, just to see me," she said. "He's tall, dark, handsome and all I want to do is put my hands on him." She lay her head back and half-moaned at the ceiling.

Mackenzie laughed. She understood it though and could feel the excitement in her building just at the idea of her best friend finally finding someone who made her so giddy.

"He asked for my number yesterday and of course, I gave it to him."

"Of course!" Mackenzie agreed.

"And now we wait for him to message, but I hope it's something saucy!"

"You would!"

"Absolutely!" She smiled widely, letting silence fall between them. It wasn't uncomfortable though, it was a sigh as they realized other things needed to be done too.

Before it could drone on long at all, Mackenzie broke the silence with a brave claim. "I'm ready to practice influencing emotions, but only with you. I don't want anyone else, not even Kai. You're the one I trust and can trust most in this world to tell me when I'm going too far or chickening out, and there's no ulterior motive with you."

"You mean, because you and Kai would get side-tracked like last time and fuck each other instead?"

"How did you... what?"

"The walls are definitely not soundproof and the next time you two do it in the living room, can you make sure I'm not home?"

Mackenzie's mouth opened wide as she stared horrified at her best friend, who laughed at the expression. Mackenzie knew Lucy was only slightly annoyed but the sheer embarrassment she might die from was very strong and real. "I'm so sorry."

"It's fine, just don't let it happen again." She laughed with a sigh. "But I accept being your emotional guinea pig. Shall we begin?"

"You going to finish your sandwich first?"

"Oh, yes!" Lucy said, quickly scooping up the second perfect half of her sandwich and shoving it in her mouth as she headed to the living area to find a seat.

Mackenzie followed, her eyes still wide from the revelation about her friend being all too aware of her sex life, and took a seat on the couch opposite her, gripping the arms of the couch.

Suddenly, the bravery she'd had before regarding her magic faded, replaced by a nervousness that chewed in her gut. "What emotion or feeling do I pick?" she said, her muscles stiff as a board as she weighed up how best to approach this.

"I could do with a nap," Lucy said, lying out on the couch in front of her like it was a psychologist's therapy lounge and she was ready for her session.

The pure ridiculousness of the image cracked Mackenzie up, the laugh spurting from her lips like a spit-take drink she was losing control of. Just like that, Mackenzie knew that everything in their magic session together would be okay. Lucy had immense trust that Mackenzie wouldn't hurt or injure her, and Mackenzie could trust that Lucy was wholeheartedly invested in helping her magic improve.

Her tight chest slowly let the air in little by little more until she was breathing deeply again. "Be serious," Mackenzie said, and Lucy lifted her hands up in surrender. On the couch, though, it only made her look like a puppy begging for belly rubs, and the laugh burst forth from Mackenzie unrestricted.

"I am…" Lucy said, grinning before she let it slide down to a comfortable seriousness a moment later. "Okay, fine, have a look through first and then you can start manipulating."

Mackenzie followed Lucy's suggestion, thankful to start with something she was comfortable with.

With a nod, Mackenzie shuffled herself further back on the couch until her back was straight against the cushions, breathing steadily and crossing her legs. She placed her hands lightly on her knees and met Lucy's gaze unflinchingly. Pushing out with her emotional awareness, she followed the warm, content feelings of her best friend who lay on the couch, her head turned to Mackenzie attentively watching her at work.

Lucy's emotional aura soothed parts of Mackenzie as she searched the surface soup of feelings, no hidden threads of concern, doubt or trepidation. It emboldened her to wade in further with her magic, a soft smile pulled her lips as she met more warmth that surrounded her like a relaxing bath. Being in Lucy's mood atmosphere was a great place to be, even as she moved into the less immediate feelings that would only rear their heads at random triggers, always subconsciously near the surface. For Mackenzie, these subconscious emotions were anxious and nerve-filled, ready to surprise her at inconvenient times. But as Mackenzie dove into Lucy's, they were like fairy-floss, a light, positive collection with very little darkness inside, the happiness and confidence melding with hunger and horniness, the closest things Lucy had to ever-present 'negative' emotions.

It was a whole new way of living, one Mackenzie hadn't been aware she was missing.

Slowly, she retreated with a smile as she became aware of Lucy watching her, grinning back.

"Like what you found?" Lucy quipped, her grin growing as her emotions sparked with a playfulness that pulled Mackenzie's lips wider.

"Absolutely! I never realized how thoroughly positive you are, Luce. It's amazing."

"Stop fanning my ego and start manipulating." Lucy laughed breathily, disbelief rising to the surface of her aura - as if she wasn't sure she believed what Mackenzie was saying but enjoyed it anyway.

Mackenzie rolled her eyes and refocused, hyper-tuned to Lucy's rolling emotions despite pulling out from the deep level.

They had never really needed the emotional magic to understand what the other was feeling, the bond they had forged over the years and true understanding of each other's persons had made sure of that. And yet, Mackenzie was happy at the new level of understanding she had of her best friend.

"Why don't we try tiredness for the emotion test?" Lucy suggested, bringing Mackenzie back to the task at hand as her mind moved for yet another tangent. "You can see the physical results easily on me and if you knock me out, it's not likely to injure me. I know you'll be careful regardless, but this way you can see it working and it's a fairly harmless feeling to play with compared to others."

Mackenzie knew what emotions Lucy meant by the waggle of her eyebrows that ended her reasoning, and memories of her getting sidetracked with Kai came to mind. Feeling how strong his attraction to her was felt intimate, powerful and all-consuming when they began to act on it.

Shaking the tangent thought from her head, she nodded to Lucy with a tight smile, agreeing with her logic. Her fingers danced with each other as she fought the urge to pick at her cuticles. "Tired, it is. Okay. I appreciate you tr-"

"Don't stall this, KZ," Lucy cut in, knowing that she was procrastinating. "Rip the plaster off or you'll talk yourself out of it."

She had to stay on track, forcing herself into action as she slipped easily back into the depths of Lucy's feelings and searched for tiredness, finding it only in the deepest corners of the subconscious soup.

For a moment, she fought to remember the way Teo had described influencing emotions, figuring his approach was the easiest to interpret. He'd described it as instinctual – that to influence an emotion, it was similar to acknowledging your own emotional regulation. The more you focused on it and let it come to life, the more it grew, like fanning the flames of a fire.

She followed the tired feeling in Lucy's aura, focusing on it and willing it to ever so slowly and carefully expand, covering the other beautiful emotions inside her best friend. She zoned out gazing into Lucy's eyes, unable to concentrate on both at the same time, switching focus between what she was seeing and the emotional aura rapidly to keep tabs on the state of her test subject. She could feel the tiredness growing, becoming more immediate and less subconscious, hearing the yawn escape Lucy's throat before acknowledging the droopiness of her friend's eyelids.

The more immediate the emotion became, the less focus Mackenzie had to dedicate to growing it and more attention she dedicated to watching the change in her friend's body.

Lucy blinked a couple of times, each close becoming longer until eventually she shut her eyes and didn't open them.

Before Mackenzie could panic, she heard the heavy, even breathing of her best friend, easing any doubt she had that she'd caused her any harm or injury. For a moment, she waited, holding the blanket of tiredness over her friend's emotional aura until she was sure it had worked properly. Then she retreated, surprised to find it staying in place, her friend resting peacefully on the couch.

Mackenzie watched for any warning signs, anything beyond the calm on her friend's face, finding a soft smile pull her lips as she observed before feeling the drain the test had taken on her magic.

Her physical state wasn't much better, all the work she'd done at martial arts, arguing with Kai and using her new magic like a physical greasy weight pressing on her shoulders. She *needed* a shower.

She stood up from the couch, contemplating if she should wake her friend – but thought better of it. They'd all been working so hard lately, pretty much since she'd left Oregon, and they all deserved a break. While it was very obvious they weren't going to get one for a long time without sacrificing a lot, for now, she let her friend enjoy the peaceful rest she was currently in.

Climbing the stairs was a feat unto itself, each step a drain on her already-fading physical ability. Her muscles were stiffening after the exercise she'd done, struggling to lift each leg as the inside of her thighs and the back of her legs complained with each movement. The entirety of her body was on fire as she pushed herself further up the stairs, knowing the shower would do wonders for her dying muscles, but it was a pain she hadn't prepared for.

11: THE TEMPTRESS

Mackenzie wasn't sure how long she'd been standing under the water. It had gradually migrated to scorching temperatures that would have boiled most others, but she was ensuring the mountains of sweat slid down the drain. Her muscles thanked her for the immense heat though, melting the stiffness that was threatening to settle in her body. At least for the moment under the torrent of water, she could pretend her body wasn't about to give up on her.

She leaned forward, pressing her forehead against the tiled wall, letting the water hit the base of her neck and run down her spine, soothing her nervous system even more.

Maybe I could stay here forever... Just hide away in here and never get out of the heavenly shower. This is all I need. Surely.

At the stupidly logical thought of the water bill cost if she did, she pulled her head back up and let the water hit her face, her eyes shut against the heat that flushed her as penance for her silly daydream.

The door creaked open and Mackenzie turned to the noise, spotting Kai as he moved inside the door, softly closing it behind himself, leaning against it. He watched her silently for a moment and she waited with raised eyebrows, letting her face ask for the update she knew was coming.

"I spoke to Matt and apologized," he said finally as his eyes scanned her naked body through the glass. He paused, and she sensed the validation he was craving, but grinned, not daring to give him the satisfaction.

"Well, isn't that nice of you," she said, letting the sarcasm thicken her voice as she shook her head, disbelieving that *this* was what he wanted her to be proud of. Brushing it off quickly and focusing on something else, she let him stew on his thoughts. She knew he was watching her attentively, clocking every tiny movement as she pressed the soap dispenser on the little shelf beside her, lathered soap between her hands and finally stepped back away from the water and slid the bubbles along her torso. She skated her hands across the top of her chest, just below the collarbone, one hand creeping into a near chokehold as she checked his expression.

His eyes didn't meet her gaze as they followed, exploring with the soap around the full extent of her breasts, washing under them. Lifting slightly, she pressed the full weight of them together as she cleaned down the sides of them. Her thumbs traced the tops of her nipples, already hardening under his gaze.

She grinned as she felt the arousal in Kai growing and the low moan that escaped his lips as she lifted them, stepping under the water and letting them drop, the weight pulling on her upper body slightly but sending a shock of excitement to her from Kai's emotional aura as she tuned in to his feelings. The moan dragged on longer, sounding near pained.

She turned to Kai, eyes wide feigning innocence as he sank further against the door, his cock already hardening in his pants. As her upper body turned, she let her elbow connect with the end of the razor hanging off the shower shelf beside her, hearing it clatter to the floor of the shower.

"What's wrong, sweetie?" she asked as she turned to give him an angle, her head still craned around to watch his reaction as she bent her upper body the full way to the floor to collect the razor she had "dropped", her ass bared to his view.

'You need to be very careful doing that…" he said, his voice thickened as he fought to swallow the warning growl in his words.

She lifted slowly, taking her time as she tried to keep the air of naivety about her. "Why's that?"

"Because if you're not careful, the wind might change and you'll stay that way," he said, his eyes narrowing as he met her gaze, his voice low and guttural. A delicious warning.

"Maybe you shouldn't be here watching then," she replied as she finally returned to standing, placing the razor back on the shelf and collecting more soap, lathering it in her hands as she spoke.

"No?

"No. You might need to go wait your turn elsewhere."

"Or we could share a shower and save on the water usage," he said, earning a scoff of amusement from Mackenzie. They both knew no water would be saved if he got into the shower with her.

"That won't do. I'm having too much fun on my own," she grinned, sliding her soapy hands in and out from between her thighs, close enough to the heat between her legs that on an occasion or two she knocked her folds with the corner of her fingers and felt the heat in her cheeks.

Kai groaned, pushing off the door and moving towards her.

She washed the soap off her body, fully aware that she'd pushed him far enough to snap. There was barely a shuffle of clothing before he stepped into the shower behind her as she watched the bubbles slide off her skin in the powerful jet of water pressing down on her.

Kai's body towered over her from behind, the hard length of him pressing into the small of her back, robbing her of breath as the feel of him ready against her zapped like electricity in her body. The pressure of him against her back pushed her forward, making sure she had to brace her hands on the wall not to bump her face into the cold tile wall below the showerhead.

His mouth bent to her neck, where the hot water melted her skin and muscle into jelly, and he used his teeth to bend the muscle to his will, drawing a moan from her lips before she could check herself.

"You going to put me out of my misery?" he whispered, barely audible over the sound of the water as his hands rested on either hip, drawing lazy circles with his thumbs.

Closing her eyes and enjoying the feel of his body against hers for a moment, she smiled, glad the hot water was helping to flush her face to hide how his touch made her heat internally. "I don't know what you're talking about," Mackenzie responded, her breathiness giving her away as she tried to continue her innocent act. "I'm just having a shower."

"Oh yeah, you're perfectly innocent in all this," he mumbled as one of his hands moved to the front of her hip, drawing a line up and down the front of her thigh, creeping ever closer to between her legs, her muscles twitching under his touch.

"Absolutely," she whispered again, knowing she had no fight in her to push him away, her breath hitching as his fingertips found the front of her, his touch so light she almost wouldn't notice if she hadn't been so in tune with exactly where every point of connection lay between them. "I don't know what you think you're doing. I'm just trying to get clean."

"And with me around you might get dirty?"

His hand crept down between her thighs, touches ever so light as he toyed with her, glancing scrapes at her opening and along the insides of her thighs. She held her breath, her eyes still shut as she held herself away from the wall she wanted to lean against as he pounded into her, but she waited, trying to fight what she knew she wanted and hold on to making him wait as teasing payback. "Well, I certainly won't get any cleaner, will I?" she tried to say, barely getting the words out.

"You really want me to leave and wait my turn?" he finally asked, a sole finger curving up inside her, eliciting a half-cry, half-gasp as she fought the noises that wanted to give him the satisfaction and fully unleash the beast in him.

"We can't…" she started, but couldn't release any other words, and started to question even her reasons for denying the absolute need she had to let him inside and ignore the world in his arms.

He paused, his finger hesitating inside her as he drawled. "Why not?"

"Because… Lucy is…" she stammered, feeling his finger playfully move inside her each time she tried to speak, stopping her short as her lower abdomen muscles tensed and her breathing became tight. She could feel the cry on the tip of her tongue.

"Still asleep on the couch," he finished the thought for her, his finger ramping up speed, her breathing coming heavier as she tried not to give him the satisfaction of hearing her cry out and hyper-aware that her sounds might wake up Lucy right after she'd been told to be careful of noise by her best friend. "I'm assuming that is your doing?"

"We were practicing…" she tried, a small cry shaking her as he stuck a second finger in her opening.

"Well, you did a very good job. She's fast asleep, so you don't have to worry about her," he reassured her, his arousal surrounding her like a warm bath, adding to the fire inside her that longed to burn as bright as he could fan it.

"I'm not exactly good at being quiet when you…"

"When I…?"

"When you fuck me."

The raspy growl in response made her insides tighten

around his finger and he pulled her hip tighter against his body, his length angling lower, sliding between her legs, skirting the opening as he gathered the liquid along it.

"If noise is all you're worried about, love, I can definitely fix that," he said, and Mackenzie could hear the grin in his tone as he moved his hips away slightly, running the shaft of him between her legs, teasing her again.

"And my sore, sweaty muscles? You going to work around those too?" Mackenzie joked as his fingers retreated from inside, and trailed their way up her body, washed by the water that slipped down her front between her breasts. They didn't stop on their journey until they rested just below her chin, lifting her head as his other hand guided her to turn around, shifting his hips to allow her the space to move.

She followed his guidance, facing him, their bodies pushing together as though they couldn't be close enough. The water now fought to escape as it flowed over her shoulders, trying to find paths between their heavily breathing bodies, pooling in places as it struggled to find spaces between their skin. His skin heated against hers – already incredibly hot from the scorching water – and yet the places they touched were like fire to her, igniting the arousal that clenched everything inside her so tightly she thought she might reach her climax just off his embrace alone.

Kai's fingertip under her chin lifted it to meet his gaze before sliding further until his hand rested lightly around the hollow of her throat, taunting her, flirting with the chokehold she knew he wasn't against using. Her lips parted slightly as her gaze flickered between his eyes and the wrist of the hand that held her throat, near daring him to do it. Instead, he held her there, and leaned his face down to meet hers, lips soft and light against hers.

She was more insistent, determined than him. While

Kai clearly was trying to tease, only allowing her little tastes of his lips brushing against hers, she raised herself on tiptoes, attempting to get closer and take control. She felt him smile against her as both hands slid down her sides, cupping her bare butt as she circled her arms up and around his neck. She couldn't get close enough as she pushed for more and more of his embrace, his kiss, his skin against hers – the closer the better as her toes complained about the height they were being pushed to.

She didn't care. He straightened his spine, her arms pulling her up off the ground as she refused to drop them from around his neck, and followed his lead as his hands swept lower than her butt, collecting her legs and guiding them to wrap highly around his waist.

A small gasp escaped as her mouth opened against his, the tip of him pressed right near her opening, pressing but not entering. He held her up though as she tried uselessly to drop her center of gravity onto him. His breathy laugh inside their mouths at her impatience only had her attempting it more.

She groaned as he held her higher, lifting her so that her neck met his lips and he bit down hard. She cried out, immediately reigning her own noise in as he shushed her and she remembered her own comment. "Not doing a very good job at keeping me quiet…" she whispered as his tongue lashed out over the place he'd bitten, soothing it.

"I haven't started yet. Didn't think you'd get so excited so quickly."

"Maybe you should start then?"

"Maybe I should…" he agreed, his voice a whisper against her ear as he pulled back, trailing his teeth playfully on her earlobe as he moved, slowly dropping her onto the tip of him again, holding her there. "You get a choice today, I'll look after you *and your noises,* but do you want it using my mouth or…?" he asked, his eyes indicating down to where his length pried her open ever so slightly, enough to make her shiver.

She considered for a moment, but she ached for him to lower her weight on to him with the hot water streaming over the backs of her shoulders, everything inside and out heated like a furnace.

"I think your mouth… is a little bit… occupied," she answered, pressing kisses between her words as she made her point clear, trying to lower herself on to him, groaning as he held her there. She waited, thinking that maybe he had some magical play in mind. Drawing back only enough to meet his eyes without crossing her own, she searched his face for the reason behind the wait. "Do you need me to conjure something?"

"No. Just you and me… No magic or extra sprinkles. Just me inside you, showing you how much I love you."

"Then what are you waiting for?" she whispered a breath away from his lips, biting her own as she leaned back slightly to ensure he caught the movement. She felt the animalistic flash of electric arousal through his emotional aura and then she was dropping.

The impact inside her as gravity drove her down on him had her crying out without restraint; only Kai's hand lightning-fast anticipating the noise and covering her mouth stopped what she was sure would have alerted anyone in a mile radius to what was happening.

He grinned as her head tipped back and she tightened around him, the muscles in her lower abdomen ignoring the tiredness of exercise from earlier as they contracted and claimed his length in their ecstasy, refusing to let him leave.

His length pulsed deeper as he listened for her early release, his supporting hand tightening into a fist under her as he held her weight against him. Turning them both, he pressed her back against the tiled wall in time for her legs to tighten then loosen their grip as pleasure rippled through her.

"Looks like your mouth might be occupied," he said roughly, staring at the hand that covered her mouth tightly, not releasing as he slid away out of her only to press deep inside her again. Her eyes rolled as he angled himself perfectly to hit the spot that had her moaning against his hand again.

He pulled himself out slightly and pounded her, again finding the spot.

And again.

And again.

Each time, eliciting a cry against his hand that sat snug around her mouth, driving harder with each noise she fought to release.

Faster and harder despite how her body clenched to hold him at his deepest.

She barely moved or slid against the tiled wall, his strong arm holding her in place as he drove again and again, the sound of slapping flesh on flesh as he pounded into her, nearly driving her over the edge. She could tell by his intensity and the way his breathing became hoarse and heavy that at any moment he would find his release inside her - and she craved it.

"Fuck, you feel so good wrapped around me, Kenz."

"I love you." She gasped as his fingers loosened slightly. She was surprised she could even speak with how breathless his thrusts were making her, crushing everything inside her with the help of gravity forcing her onto the full eight inches of him.

He pressed his fingers down again, his pace somehow increasing at her words.

She found her release, tightening more than she thought her body was capable of as she tipped her head back to the tile and her eyes unseeingly rolled up under her eyelids.

And like her ecstasy was tied to his, she felt him ripple inside her and finish with her, his face burying in her neck as he went still beneath her.

His hand slid from her mouth to hold the other side of her neck from where he held his face, supporting her head as the adrenaline left her body and she sank into the wall. The sound of the water running down the drain and their heavy breathing were the only sounds filling the room in the aftermath of their love.

12: THE KIDNAPPER'S CHOICE

Mackenzie had finally exited the shower after spending the next age cuddled up against Kai under the stream of hot water - unsure her legs would hold her after the bruising he'd given her organs – to find a text from Matt on her phone. It was cryptic and vague but gave her a sense of hope about the new day that had dawned.

She'd barely slept that night, still unable to think about anything other than the text:

BE GLAD TOMORROW IS THE BEGINNING OF THE SPRING SEMESTER. I FOUND THE LEAD WE NEED TO FOLLOW TO FIND YOUR MOTHER. MEET ME OUTSIDE THE ENTRANCE BY THE ROAD AT 9:30 AM. I'LL EXPLAIN EVERYTHING THEN.

Despite the lack of sleep, she felt invigorated, adrenaline coursing through her veins as she stepped off the bus and headed over to a nearby tree to wait the twenty minutes for Matt to arrive. She wasn't sure what to expect: every single question response begging for more information had gone unanswered, left on read. She brought her items for classes that day in her backpack in case their search was a dead end or didn't take up all her time and she had to wait; if it came down to that, she would need a distraction. She was itching to bring her mom home already.

She waited, bouncing on her toes and staring at the

pile of texts she had left in Matt's inbox, uncaring if he thought it was too much. Everything inside her buzzed with a readiness to see all of this over. She didn't even try to fight to keep her body still as she continuously checked the clock until finally, she caught sight of the brown hair stepping out of the Jeep nearby. Only then did she fight her body's innate anxious desires and not bound over to him with millions of questions.

His face held little of the light-hearted humor she had seen in his angular features before, contemplative and thoughtful as he sauntered over to where she stood.

Only once he was mere feet away from her did she finally decide to speak, making sure that the students that filtered into the building around them were outside of earshot. "You finally going to explain what we're doing?" Watching him nod and compile the words in his head before he spoke, she reached out to his emotional aura, sensing the calm he seemed to press down on himself as though he was convincing himself to relax. Under the surface, it was a boiling pot of anxiety making her sick to her stomach to feel.

"The weak link of the Arcana. I have intel that one of the 'lesser' members is Lily Valentina."

"Gosh, now I hear that full name out loud I should've realized it was fake," Mackenzie blurted, watching the edges of his mouth pull up slightly at the ends. It was only there for a moment as he refocused on the task at hand though, and the heavy seriousness returned to his face.

Her stomach twisted sharply as she felt his false guise of serenity harder to maintain hiding the anxiety in his aura. He was losing the ability to convince himself and it would show soon.

"Lily's family belongs to the Empress tarot bloodline."

"And what's that power?"

"Control of nature," he said, and Mackenzie began to understand the sheer anxiety in him.

The idea of going up against someone with control of

nature, whatever the full extent of that meant, was sweat-inducing. *How do I fight against that?* "That doesn't like 'lesser' to me."

"Well, the caveat is that she has to be in sight of nature to use it. So if she's inside a building…"

"Her power is useless," Mackenzie finished with a guess, earning his nod of confirmation, the churning feeling in her gut subsiding slightly as she realized Lily wasn't all-powerful.

"Correct. The Empress's bloodline definitely doesn't have the strength or versatility of the Emperor's powers. It's only the status of the two that has them treated similarly inside the Arcana."

"So they have the same secrets, even though one is vastly more powerful than the other?"

"Exactly," he said, his face smoothing as she clarified – somehow calming his own fears as she verified for herself.

"And do you know who has the Emperor's powers?" she asked, her chest tight as she hoped for an answer, holding her breath as she checked his expression.

"We do not, that's a well-protected secret we haven't been able to discover yet."

The breath sighed out of her. "Damn. So, what's the plan here?" She checked around them again, thankful for their placement off the path and the cooler temperatures driving the other students all inside.

"We corner Lily and use necessary means to extract answers," Matt responded, his voice barely louder than a whisper as he stepped closer to her.

Mackenzie's eyes widened as her spine straightened jarringly. "Necessary means?"

"You have the Fool's bloodline powers now, don't you? Kai mentioned you'd been practicing how to use them," he continued, answering his own questions but not soothing any of her surprise.

"I haven't mastered them! And what if something goes wrong?"

"And what if it doesn't? There's no time like the present to master it," he said quickly, checking his watch, and walked off, apparently expecting her to follow.

Mackenzie stood for a moment, the surprise still holding her body. Her mouth dropped open as though she'd give him a response. He was already well out of earshot by the time her mouth could even make any more sounds through her surprise. She recovered enough to hurry after him, catching up after a few jogging steps and slowing as she reached him.

She needn't have bothered slowing down though: Matt speed-walked in the building and through the corridors, his long legs propelling him quicker than her legs could walk comfortably. He didn't slow or check behind him as he moved, glancing between his watch and the corridor in front of him as he raced until finally he stopped in front of one of the lecture halls, pulling her away from the students that filtered in, and whispering, "One of the guys works in the administration office and mentioned Lily's first class of the day was this one. You're going to lure her away for a quick chat in this empty room, we're going to grab her and ask her some questions. She won't be able to use her powers in the building with no plants around, and you can use your new powers to keep her compliant." The nerves that had been pushing around inside him calmed to preparedness at the explanation his own plan.

"You've really thought a lot about this," she noted, watching the way his shoulders pushed back and he stood taller at her validation.

"What can I say? I'm a planner. And I've been waiting for an excuse to get involved in all the action," he said quickly with a small smile, finally seeming more like the everyday self she was beginning to learn.

Mackenzie tried to return the smile but felt the full burden of what he was planning for her to do like a physical weight pressing uncomfortably on her shoulders, as though it was lopsided and misshaped as it leant on her. "This is a lot really quickly!" She breathed out before she could think on her words and watched his face drop in response as he stepped closer to her, one hand taking her shoulder in his hand.

"Hey, you want your mom back, yes?"

"Of course!" she responded instinctively, watching his face unsurprised by her response.

"Then what are you willing to do to get her back?"

As if it were that simple and nothing else mattered.

She stood back, her weight sinking into her heels as she stared blankly back at Matt. He seemed to be waiting for her answer, but in the silence as she thought about his question, it seemed answer enough for her.

"I'm willing to do it," she said, watching as the response appeased him and he hurried across the hall from her.

With a nod, he opened the door to the empty room and disappeared inside it, leaving her to decide how she wanted to get Lily away from her lecture.

Mackenzie peered inside the lecture hall, slowly filling with students - thankfully no sign of Lily yet.

She didn't have long to think as the champagne orange hair with easy loose curls flicked its way down the hallway. Mackenzie stuck with the first solid idea that jumped in her head. She knew the moment Lily had noticed her by the way she froze mid-step. Mackenzie tried to tune in to the emotions coming off the Empress's aura, shock and confusion on the surface and irritation flickering in its wake.

"Mackenzie?" Lily blurted, clutching her laptop close to her chest as she finally began walking towards the lecture hall – and Mackenzie – again.

"Oh my god, Lily!" Mackenzie shrieked, leaning into the shaky nervousness that wracked her body at the sight of the girlfriend of the woman who'd stabbed her. She wasn't sure whether Lily shared her paramore's need for blood, so she stood just enough away – even in public – to avoid any surprises. "I'm so glad I found you here! I need to talk to you! I'm worried about what he's going to do to her!"

"What who's going to do to *who*?" Lily reeled, panic flashing in her aura.

Internally, Mackenzie triumphed, spinning the story as she went, letting her voice shake. "Kai!" Mackenzie whispered as Lily finally got close enough. Looking around cautiously, Mackenzie tried to make a point of hiding her panic as she glanced at the other entrants to the lecture hall who glanced over curiously at her outburst. "I'm worried about what he's going to do to Amari!"

"Why would he do anything to Amari?" Lily blinked quickly as she tried to follow along with the words Mackenzie was throwing at her.

"He finally thought he had a shot at getting back at her…" Mackenzie leaned in quickly, whispering the second part for emphasis as her eyes wandered away for any onlookers. "…for what she did to *me*."

Lily breathed in sharply at the mention of the incident that had ended up with Mackenzie in hospital with a stab wound in her abdomen, as though invoking that event had somehow made it seem as though she were telling the truth. The sharp confusion and shock muted in Lily's aura, being consumed by an overwhelming heart-wrenching panic as she worried for the safety of her girlfriend.

Mackenzie was almost moved to feel sorry for her. *Almost.*

Once more, Mackenzie glanced sharply at a girl who lingered outside the lecture hall, Lily following her gaze and moving slightly away from the lecture hall towards the empty room Mackenzie needed her in. "Can we go somewhere…private…to talk?" Mackenzie stammered, looking around as though she were searching for the answer before walking up to the room she knew Matt had disappeared into. Putting her hand on the doorknob and glancing back at Lily, she waited for her to move closer before she opened the door, indicating for her confidant to go first.

"Of course!" Lily didn't hesitate with her response, hurrying through with quick clicky steps as her small blocky heels struck the tiles, grip loosening on her laptop as she made it through the doorway, Mackenzie rushing behind her to shut the door before anyone could see the scene about to unfold.

Matt didn't hesitate the moment the door hid the view to the public: he appeared from the wall beside the door, snatching the laptop and skimming it away along the floor, before grabbing both Lily's wrists and yanking them behind her back.

Lily tried to struggle, but Mackenzie acted on the first thing she could think of, conjuring cable ties and leaning forward to tighten them around Lily's joined wrists above Matt's grip. She didn't shy from making sure they were taut before moving away and conjuring cloth as Matt reached the same thought, moving one of his hands to cover Lily's mouth and nose before she could scream out for help.

Backing Lily against the wall next to the door they'd just walked through, Matt looked back at Mackenzie, mildly impressed as she checked in with her magic to make sure the tie between her conjuration and power was strong and stable.

"That's a speedy manifestation trick!" he commented with a smile, and she could tell he was trying to lighten both of their anxieties as he pressed Lily back against the wall, hand over mouth as Mackenzie focused on keeping her magic strong to avoid any surprises by Lily, aware of the absolute hot fiery anger coming off her in waves, threatening to burn Mackenzie if she looked too close.

"Don't ask me why I've practiced it so much," Mackenzie breathed in response, returning the joking attitude with a half-smile, watching Lily attentively, hyper-aware of every tensing muscle. She heard the breathy quiet chuckle as Matt caught her meaning.

"Just to be clear, we need answers from you, but if you scream I have no problem returning the favor your girlfriend started last fall," Matt warned Lily as the humor dropped from his face and he conjured a knife in the hand that wasn't covering her mouth.

At the sight of the clean shiny metal in front of her view, Lily's struggling stilled and her eyes widened, the breathing through Matt's hand coming heavier and slower as she realized the severity of her situation.

The fear that laced with Lily's anger was like fuel on a fire, hurting Mackenzie as she adventured through its surface. Mackenzie's eyes widened in shock as she looked at Matt for a moment, not sure what she had expected from him, but not... that.

Refocusing on the task at hand, she returned her view to Lily, who watched Matt with the attention of a hawk.

With a deep breath, Mackenzie pushed her emotional awareness out, jumping properly into Lily's aura instead of just sensing the waves that came off her.

Despite the burning feeling that accompanied the anger, once Mackenzie pushed past it, all she felt was cold. An aura unlike anything she had expected from the quiet, bubbly woman she'd met at a party months before stood in front of her now. Icy cold hatred met her underneath the anger bubbling on the surface, with fear leaking in between. Her goal was to find something to enhance that would make Lily compliant to answering her questions, but there seemed to be nothing to focus on that would do such a thing.

"Lily," she said, watching the angry eyes of the orange-haired girl flick to her, features somehow sharper in her anger than they had been before – like Mackenzie could finally see how angry and icy she was manifested in her features, unable to be ignored. "Do you know where my mother is?"

Lily waited for a moment, anger pulsing through her,

no empathy or care for the woman who asked her questions, worried for her family – no emotion for Mackenzie to grip on to. Lily nodded, a cruel smile pulling what Mackenzie could see of her lips. Matt slid his fingers away slowly and warily, ready to return them at a moment's notice.

"Will you tell me?" Mackenzie pleaded, trying again to convey with her eyes the heartache the loss of her mother was causing her.

Lily huffed. "Nice try," she whispered snidely, glancing at the knife Matt still held in view, her hands still pressed firmly against the wall her back was pushed against. Mackenzie knew that the cable ties stayed intact and still. Lily wasn't trying to move her wrists. The hate grated on Mackenzie as she struggled, lost in Lily's aura for anything to use. "What if Amari was taken from you?" she asked, her gaze steady as she watched the flinch in Lily's angular face, temporarily softening it in worry. "You don't have to worry... I'm not taking her from you, but I just want you to think about what you'd do to get her back."

She could feel the tiniest spark of humanity in Lily, a stream of love for her girlfriend hiding in amongst the immense cold and hot anger and hostility. Before it could disappear, Mackenzie latched on it, focusing on the feeling and giving it life. She made sure that amongst it she held on to her own willpower, keeping it tied to the cable ties around Lily's wrists, and instantly felt the drain of two magics working at the same time – something she'd make a note to practice later. "I think I have it," she whispered to Matt, her eyes staying trained, unseeing, on Lily's eyes.

"Alright, Lily..." Matt said quietly, as though speaking too loud would shatter the concentration and power Mackenzie was now confident she held over Lily.

Taking over the question-asking from Mackenzie was a great idea – one she was thankful for, unsure how many things she'd be able to focus on at once, if she had to ask the right questions too.

"Who holds the power of the Emperor?"

The feelings that unexpectedly shot through Lily's emotions were like a bullet through Mackenzie's mind. It went from entire control, fanning love over all her other emotions, to sheer panic and fear, a wall coming down between their connection. And like a quick-shut garage door as Mackenzie still reached through into Lily's aura, the pain that reverberated through her magic made Mackenzie keel over her knees, crying out. She tried to hold in the noise but felt all her magic grip slipping at the pain, her hands reaching to her temples as though it could stop it all.

By the time she'd recovered from the blinding flash of pain, Matt and Lily had moved – Lily's hands now free from the cable tie that had faded from existence, Matt recovering the upper hand by bracing his arm across her chest to hold her against the wall and lifting the bejeweled knife to her throat.

Mackenzie took a deep breath, straightening up as her brain returned to normal.

Lily's face had once again returned to the angry darkness from before the glimmer of humanity.

"This isn't going to work, Matt," Mackenzie said breathily, wiping the sheen of sweat from her forehead.

"We can't let her go back to the Arcana. They'll retaliate," he replied, waiting for further ideas as it was clear he'd run out of them.

Once again, Mackenzie was left just to go with the best idea that occurred to her the fastest. She could remake her connection to Lily's aura, but she doubted she'd be able to find the nugget of emotion she'd found before. So she did the only thing she could think of in that moment that would save her from further issue: she found the little tired feeling in the back of Lily's emotional aura and focused on that quicker than she'd tried before.

Lily's body slumped slightly in response and luckily,

123

Matt realized what was happening right before it did. The knife pulled from Lily's throat just in time for her whole body to slide down to the floor, eyes closed and breathing serene and deep.

Both Mackenzie and Matt stood back, looking at how calm Lily looked as she slept on the tiled floor.

"What now?" Matt asked.

"Now we find a way to get her back to my place where she becomes my hostage until I get the answers I want," Mackenzie found herself answering, surprising even herself with the words that slipped out.

Matt nodded slowly as he turned his head to look at Mackenzie as though he were looking at a new person; she couldn't quite tell if he respected this new girl or not. "Okay, I can make that happen. You should get to class though."

"What?" she snapped, drawing back and looking at him as though he'd grown two heads.

"The Arcana watches you very closely. If they notice Lily goes missing today, they'll check you first. I'm sure of it. The Order will get her to your house without being seen, you will be noticed if you don't go to your first class of the semester," he explained, ducking off quickly to hide the laptop he'd skimmed across the floor under one of the chairs of the lecture hall they stood in.

He made sense – she hated to admit it – and she took a deep breath, acknowledging that she probably needed to take his advice, especially since her first class might just be with Amari.

She couldn't give that woman fuel for any anger. Mackenzie wasn't sure what Amari would do to her if she suspected her of kidnapping her girlfriend, but it would be so much worse than what she'd done in the name of the Arcana last fall.

Mackenzie moved away from Lily, holding on to the straps of her backpack, shuffling reluctantly towards the door, looking up at Matt for reassurance.

"I'll get it done. You can trust me, Mac," he said

softly, nodding at her to leave the situation with him.

Before she could regret her decision, she unlocked the door, and ducked out into the hallway heading off in the direction of what she was sure would be a painstakingly long hour of anxiety.

13: THE DOWNWARD SPIRAL

Not only had Mackenzie fried and tired every nerve in her body from sitting through an hour two seats away from Amari, who was clearly still blissfully unaware that her girlfriend had disappeared from the Arcana's reach, but she'd also had to endure two more classes, one of which had been with Teo – who had continually glanced at her, still not recognizing her but obviously remembering the odd confrontation from his house.

He kept trying to watch her as though he could rejog his memory just from the length of time he looked at her.

All through this, she was somehow meant to focus on classes, take notes and prepare herself for another semester of learning – and not let her marks suffer like they had last semester. She was surprised she'd even passed at all last semester with the chaos she'd endured.

And so, it seemed, she was destined to do it all again.

Mackenzie unlocked the front door of her house, feeling the anxiety, temper and mixed negative emotions swirling on the other side of it. She contemplated turning around and going to lie down on a park bench somewhere just to escape it for a little while; she had enough negative emotions of her own without being yelled at by everyone else's.

But this was the safest place for her to be right now and she was hoping to get answers to find her mother.

The quicker she did, the sooner she could release Lily, get her mom back and hopefully find some normalcy to her life.

As if that's likely, she found herself scoffing, making her pause on the doorknob as she considered the thought. *What if it never ends?*

She trembled at the idea that this fear, panic and anxiety caused by an organization like the Arcana coming after her would last forever. It wasn't sustainable and surely it would kill her quicker than she could outrun it.

Before she could stew on the idea too long, she opened the door and pushed inside, unprepared for the chaos that met her.

Matt, Kai and Lucy all stood in the living room arguing.

"Oh, and whose brilliant idea was it to start taking hostages? That wasn't what we talked about!" Kai snapped, his fury like fireworks against her skin as she gripped her backpack straps tightly, her nails pushing into the thick fabric painfully.

"It was mine," she said loudly, snapping them from their deep conversation to her presence.

Kai's face fell as he looked over at her, recognition of her words dawning on her face. "Why?" His voice dropped in volume as he realized whose choice it was he was now questioning.

"You didn't see in her aura what I did. Very little of her had any humanity or goodness and it wasn't viable to keep trying to pry her for information onsite," Mackenzie explained, having practiced her logical reasoning on the way home in her head, fully aware Kai would question it. How much he would continue to do so, she wasn't sure. "Plus, if we gave up then, Matt was sure the Arcana would retaliate on us whether we got the information from Lily or not. At least now we have the time to collect the actual information we want and act on it before they hear it was us."

127

"That's nuts! They'll know it was you the second they realize she's missing!" he retorted, but it didn't stir any anxiety in her as she met Matt's gaze.

Matt nodded his confirmation that he had managed what he'd promised without a hiccup and she faced Kai again, confident and sure. "They won't!" she said.

"And how can you be sure?"

"Because I just sat through three hours of class while she was missing with Amari and Teo. Dealing with them in my lectures was my alibi."

Kai's face smoothed out, warm concern flushing his emotional aura as he stepped closer to her. "Are you okay?" he asked softly, and the insides of her heated soothingly at his question.

She nodded slightly with a calm little smile to reassure him. "It was hard but I did it and I'm okay, I promise."

He waited a moment, searching her face for any sign to the contrary before realizing her confidence in her answer, nodding alongside her as he accepted the new premise. "We just need to remember that we're not them and we're better than that," he said, the softness in his tone non-threatening and non-accusatory as he spoke.

"Are we?" she said before she could question her own motives, feeling the implication in his words like a personal attack. It had been her idea to bring Lily here and it was her home she was incapacitated in. She glanced around as though she could spot the new occupant from her vantage point, but Kai interrupted her eye wanderings before she could leave the room to search in person.

"What do you mean?"

"What would you do if it had been me taken?" she asked, taking the way his face darkened dangerously in response as an answer. She waited as her point sunk in, and his anger that he was trying to hide beneath the surface – because he didn't want to be angry at *her* –

cooled off.

She turned to Lucy, who had clearly been irritated by the men having an argument in the room, knowing her dislike of alpha male posturing. She felt Lucy's irritation disappear as she took ownership for the ideas in the room. "What do you think of all this?" Mackenzie asked her best friend; if she thought it a bad idea, then an alternate plan should be considered. She had no other agendas or jealousy or cock-measuring to do like the men did, and Mackenzie knew the answer that slipped from between her lips would be honest enough to trust wholeheartedly.

"It's not what I would've picked, but it's probably the only good idea any of us have at the moment." Lucy sighed, surrendering as she spoke, putting any inklings of anxious doubt deep in Mackenzie to rest. "I'll back you if this is what you're choosing to do. Go get your mom back."

Mackenzie and Lucy nodded at each other, the silent respect strong between the two of them in the quiet.

Finally, Mackenzie turned to Matt, her eyebrows lifting as she waited for the information she required to begin the path she'd chosen.

"She's tied up in the basement downstairs with real restraints this time so you don't have to try and manifest at the same time as getting into her emotions," he said slowly, showing he understood some of what had happened back at the University. "I'll head off so that I'm not drawing suspicion being here often. You need to make sure you try to live your life as normally as possible in the meantime until you get the answers you need. It could take time, so…"

Her organs scrunched up uncomfortably at the idea of having to wait for answers any longer, but she nodded quietly again so he knew she understood.

"Thank you," she said quietly as he backed up towards her front door.

"Call if you need anything further," he responded,

reluctant to leave but making pointed eye contact with her.

Once he'd left, silence filled the room, neither Lucy, Mackenzie or Kai moving as the room collectively seemed to hold its breath.

Mackenzie was the first to break the stalemate.

Heading for the basement entrance, she didn't speak a word to her comrades as she opened the door and descended into the dark. She couldn't let her eagerness speed her steps as she walked, feeling her footsteps carefully down each concrete step, hearing it echo off the walls around her. She knew Kai followed her, quiet in his journey, his aura nervous but soft, knowing he was there only as observer; this was something Mackenzie had to do herself.

As she followed the basement around the corner to her wall of weapons, she tried to prepare herself for what she'd find, but still couldn't have given herself enough mental warning.

Lily was conscious in the center of the room, tied to a heavy metal chair in the same place months ago the black orb on the hilt of Mackenzie's family's sword had shattered. It had been a perfect metaphor back then for how magic would blow her life part, and now the space was filled with what she was sure was the biggest development for her since.

Metal chains secured Lily's limbs together at the ankles and wrists and wrapped tightly around her body at the chest, stomach, hips, and thighs, making sure she couldn't move from the seat. The link in the chain *clinked* softly as Lily tried to breathe deeply against the weight of her chains, looking as though she was trying to stay calm – the piece of material gagging her as her eyes found and locked onto Mackenzie. The fury was palpable even without the use of the Fool's powers.

Mackenzie caught sight of Kai as she moved around Lily. He stood back and let her take the focus of the movement, leaning against the wall as he served as her protector, should she need him.

Leaning forward, Mackenzie reached behind Lily's head carefully, slowly loosening the knot at the back of the cloth gag and pulling it from her mouth. She stayed in tune with Lily's emotions, feeling the flood of relief as Lily stretched her mouth and cheeks out, opening and closing her jaw once it was free of the cloth. Mackenzie wanted to make sure, hyper-aware, that Lily didn't suddenly yell and use this as an opportunity to cry for help.

Following Matt's example from earlier that day, Mackenzie leaned back, making unflinching eye contact with Lily as she gave her a warning threat. "Make a single attempt at calling for help and I'll make sure you don't wake up for a very long time."

Lily stayed silent, eyes narrowing as she watched her captor carefully. Mackenzie waited patiently for the verbal confirmation that she understood. None came; instead, Lily leaned her head back as though she didn't have a care in the world – as though she wasn't tied to a chair in someone's basement – and smiled cruelly at Mackenzie.

She is the perfect match for Amari, Mackenzie scoffed internally.

"You know, I remember when you first came to town. Bright-eyed and eager to find the ties to the family you were missing, willing to do anything and trust everyone for the chance to connect with that heritage and the Arcana. What happened?" Lily said, and Mackenzie was sure she just enjoyed hearing the sound of her own voice. But at least she wasn't trying to scream for help or escape.

"You all taught me how stupid that was. Trusting someone as easily as I did all of you was a game of life or death that was going to get me killed. I adapted. Now I don't play your games anymore, I've found my own rules," she said flatly, feeling the bite in her tone as she spoke, imagining it as daggers able to pierce through

Lily's skull.

It didn't manifest, it was only a vile thought she found herself indulging as she looked at the woman who stood between her and her mother's location.

What would you do to get her back? Matt's words replayed in her head, driving a darkness in her that she hadn't known before. She'd do nearly anything to get her back and that was an answer she was terrified to speak aloud.

All of this was not helped by the smug cruelty that filled Lily's aura as Mackenzie studied it, feeling herself pulling from the feelings as she was surrounded by them, hard to determine from her own self as she moved deeper.

"New rules? By following in your ancestor's footsteps and recruiting the Order of Wands? They're nice to look at but I'm not sure how much help they'll be to you."

As though she were handing her helpful advice.

"They helped capture you, didn't they?" Mackenzie returned the bitter smile as she searched deeper and deeper into Lily's feelings, trying to find a shred of something she could fan brighter and use, but nothing appeared with alarming regularity. The majority of Lily's emotions seemed to be sour and cruel, something Mackenzie knew would be incredibly hard to use to make her talk.

"You got lucky," Lily said snidely, flares of annoyance hitting Mackenzie like sparks of a fire.

Mackenzie's own anger was ready to ignite. "They're more powerful than you think, and together? We're going to take all of you down," she snapped before she could stop herself, regretting the words the moment they left her lips.

Lily's eyes widened in response, a spring of sweet delight flickering in Mackenzie's magical periphery. She snagged it before it could fade, wary not to celebrate yet as she focused on it slowly, worried it might disappear as easily as it appeared. She let the delight grow lightly, annoyed by the responses it created.

"The Arcana will be *very interested* to hear that."

"I'm sure they will be, *after* you tell me what I need to know."

"We both know that's not going to happen." Lily laughed, the surprise at Mackenzie's statement not present in her aura, only making it sound as though she thought Mackenzie was crazy.

For the answers she wanted, Mackenzie would endure it.

"Not without a fight," Mackenzie mumbled as her focus stole her ability to see more than the zoned-out shapes. She tried to make sure she had stared into space in Lily's eyes, hoping Lily wouldn't notice how utterly robbed she was by the amount of magic she was expending to make Lily more pliable.

The theory Mackenzie had decided on was that if she made Lily's cruel delight strong enough, she would rant like an evil villain until the answers fell out of her.

"So what? You're going to torture me for your information?" Lily challenged, a glimmer of fear hiding underneath the blanket of delight Mackenzie stretched over it all, muting it.

For a moment, Mackenzie considered focusing on that instead but wasn't sure how much more successful fear would be except to make Lily scared to speak. *That's Plan B*, she told herself, *if this one doesn't work.* She would try again and again to get Lily to speak until she found the answers she needed. "I don't think you realize how far I'll go to get my family back," she warned, the hatred burning inside her as she felt the trueness of that statement ring through her vocal cords.

"What would your mother think?" Lily asked innocently, posing with a smile as she turned her head on an angle.

Mackenzie zoned in to see Lily begin to notice the lack of sight she'd had, the utter focus being dedicated to something magical that was robbing her of the moment.

"I wouldn't know. She hasn't been around in a few years thanks to your organization, but I'm sure I'll figure out her thoughts after I find her. Now, where is my mother being held?"

"I don't know." Lily answered quickly and lightly, but Mackenzie had only to look at Kai's form, using the wall as a leaning post to her left, and his shaking, disappointed head to know it wasn't to be believed.

"It's a lie," he said, crushing her belief that delight was the way to tackle this. With an aggravated scream, Mackenzie's first plan fell to bits. She let go of the blanket of delight, feeling it flit away into the ether as Lily's horror at the control she'd lost overtake it.

"You bitch!" Lily said, her eyes narrowing as she sat forward as though she could leap out of the chair and collect Mackenzie on the way to the floor.

"If I have to be," Mackenzie said, conjuring a knife in her palm before she could think about it. Stepping forward, closer to the chair and their prisoner chained to it, she lifted it slightly, letting the light glint off its edge.

Lily's eyes tracked the new object, widening, her breathing hitching as fear consumed her insides, rancid and gnawing.

Mackenzie launched again, choosing this new emotion as the backup plan, and without hesitation, growing it quicker and quicker until it looked as though Lily might lose consciousness with how quickly she was breathing. That or scream.

"Where is my mother?"

"I can't tell you!"

Kai nodded from his place at the wall, indicating the truth had been spoken – even though she already knew that was the case. It was a technicality but it was correct.

"What is the location where my mother is being held?!"

"I can't tell you!" Lily yelled louder, closing her eyes, tears leaking from the corner as she tried to calm her breathing. The water left pathways down her cheeks, dragging the eye makeup in black smudges and carving streaks through her foundation.

At the sight of tears, Mackenzie's own frustration rose; if Lily expected sympathy, she was getting none from her. With a scowl, she waited, tapping her foot as she held onto the fear focus, letting it simmer with Lily and convince her to answer. But the longer it went on, Lily's limbs shaking against her chains, the more impatient Mackenzie found herself becoming.

One more step and Mackenzie pressed the tip of her knife to Lily's upper arm, watching the shock of the cold metal through Lily's long sleeve shirt shock her to stillness. Her mouth dropped open as if she might scream but no noise escaped. No answers did either.

"I'll say it one more time and you better give me an answer. *Where is my mother?*" Mackenzie asked with soft malice, letting all her fury bundle in, ready to be unleashed for the wrong answer or avoiding questions. She could see Lily prepare to repeat her same answer, so she applied slight pressure to the knife, hearing Kai voice his warning in the form of her name.

Once again, she ignored him.

"Not in Salem." Lily sobbed.

Mackenzie considered for a moment, almost tempted to accept it and withdraw the knife – but it wasn't nearly enough to begin her search, and *clearly* the knife tactic was working.

"That wasn't a good enough answer, Lily," she snapped, slipping the tip of the knife down Lily's arm with the right amount of force to slice through the shirt and surface of the skin underneath. It was deep enough to force the silent screams into sound, but not enough that Mackenzie would have to get her medical attention for stitches.

Mackenzie finally pulled the knife away when the cut became long enough to turn Lily's scream to a shriek. "Try again."

Before Lily could give her an alternate answer that satisfied, or risk another scar down the other arm, Kai's hand held Mackenzie's knife hand tightly and growled in her ear. "Out. *Now.*"

14: THE INTERROGATOR'S DARKNESS

Kai's words resonated through Mackenzie's senses as he whispered in her ear, a warning that cut through every nerve in her body.

She shivered as her magic pulled back from Lily near instantly, complying with the fury and command emanating from his entire aura. The knife in her hand disappeared as she turned her head to meet his face.

He leaned back from her ear, every feature of his face dark and serious. Moving quickly, he walked away towards the bottom of the staircase, no question that she should follow. He didn't look back, but she knew he was listening carefully to her steps as she surrendered and reluctantly scuffled along behind him.

Despite her compliance with his words, she stared daggers in his back, the base of her neck heating angrily. Each step away from her hostage seemed like a defeat, reverberating through her legs as she stomped aggressively up the concrete steps. She had to make her point to him.

The sound of Lily sobbing as she moved away and left her to her unrestrained emotions was somehow the anthem of defeat for Mackenzie.

At the top of the stairs, Kai held the door open – ever the gentleman – until she was through, then made a point of shutting the door loudly, letting it swing shut with enough force to make her jump when her back was turned.

"What the fuck was that?" he asked, breaking the tensioned silence.

Mackenzie turned violently on him at the words, the heat that had been building inside her finally exploding on him. "Don't talk to me like that!"

"Answer the question," he ordered, crossing his arms as he stood stiffly, his gaze unflinchingly boring into hers.

"I don't know what you're talking about…"

"What I saw in there, that wasn't you." His eyebrows lifted questioningly.

Her stomach burned, warming at the thought that he had any right to question, which only fuelled her anger more. "You don't understand, Kai. What I see when I look in her emotions, there's no care for other people, no empathy, no light. It's so dark in there, she-"

"I don't care how evil you think she is," he interrupted, sending Mackenzie's spine straight like a rod.

She waited with unblinking wide eyes as he continued, her mouth flinching between a grimace and a frown, unable to decide how to hold the anger that bubbled like a cauldron inside her.

"No matter what sort of darkness you see in them, or the lack of goodness in their souls and emotions, that doesn't make *torture* okay."

"You're not my parent! So fuck off and leave me to make my own choices!"

"I know I'm not your parent! I'm just the guy who's watching you give yourself up to get what you want!" he yelled back. His arms dropped and his incredulous expression grew frustratingly confused.

Whatever point he was trying to make, she wasn't getting it and she didn't care. He was wrong, she knew it. She would do whatever was required of her to get the answers and it infuriated her that he would've done the same in her position but had the audacity to question it.

"I know how far I would go to get my mom back!" she retorted.

His expression twisted as he tried to convey what he obviously thought of as her madness. "It's not about that!"

"Then what is it about?" It was her turn to cross her arms and watch him in confusion.

"It's about not torturing and kidnapping people!"

"Why not? The Arcana have proved that they are willing to do anything they want to keep my mom from me. I won't get her back unless I play by their rules!"

"There's going to be another way, Kenz!"

"You, by the way, have no leg to stand on. Not that long ago you were willing to kill Teo in the name of love for me. How is that any different?"

"I know I would kill to protect you and god knows I wanted to after what he did to you, but I didn't."

"My hero." Her voice dripped with sarcasm as she spoke, watching the angered love in him replaced by frustration as his features dropped and his eyes looked ready to roll at her words. She felt a small tinge of regret at her choice, but knew it was too late to take it back and she was too angry to really mean her apology.

Thankfully, he continued on with his point, ignoring her lapse in judgement.

"It's not about how far you're willing to go for the ones you love. That's how you learn the real depth of your feelings, sure. But being good enough for their love in return is something else entirely. Knowing where the line is is what separates us into deserving or not. You can't sacrifice your goodness in the name of your mother, or you're as bad as the Arcana."

Mackenzie scoffed.

"You can't seriously believe that! The Arcana aren't doing any of this out of love, only in the name of power."

"Does it matter what the intention is if it's producing the same result?" he asked, leaving her silent as the point he was making finally sank in.

The question both infuriated and terrified her all at once, making it feel like her entire chest cavity was hollow, just like her stomach. She stared for a moment, blinking, somehow aware that he was waiting for her retort – but she couldn't seem to find anything to say that had any merit.

His face began to change from anger to an openness that showed smugness as he began to realize he had stumped her.

She wanted to throw something at him, at the very least words that would answer his retort and not make her come off like an ignorant idiot.

The silence between them dragged on and despite feeling the anger inside him fade, she was surprised she wasn't on fire with how frustrated she was and it was only getting worse with her own silence. Only now the target of all her frustration had migrated from him, the Arcana and the world, to herself. Well, and always the Arcana as well.

With a sigh, Kai ended the stalemate between them. "Go and take some time elsewhere. Go for a run or burn it off doing something else. That anger and desperation needs to go. I get it, I do, but if you take those feelings down there you'll regret it later." Kai's voice was stern, so much so that she knew unless she went and did as he said, he would make sure she didn't enter her basement.

Her shoulders sank in defeat. "I don't want to wait for answers, Kai," she admitted slowly, watching him soften at her words as though he remembered the real reason they were all here doing this.

"I know, but you're not going to be doing your mother any good if you're pushing Lily too far and she shuts down. I promise I'll be here asking her questions while you're gone. Go and lose the restless energy."

She waited for a moment, searching his eyes for any sign that he was lying – that she'd come back from blowing off steam to find Lily gone or that he'd just taken it upon himself to torture her himself so she wouldn't have to – but his gaze was steady and there wasn't a single trace in the aura that told her she had anything to fear. He knew what her mother meant to her and despite her journey to the darker side of herself, he knew Lily was their best chance at finding Mackenzie's family.

Without another word, she turned and made her way up the stairs, dragging her feet, scuffing and almost tripping on a number of steps on her way up. As she checked her watch and the printed timetable on her desk, she pulled her new martial arts uniform from the closet.

She could use an excuse to punch something.

***

Mackenzie had never expected to spend as much time in a martial arts gym as she had already in the past month. Grant never seemed to invest in heating the space, and she wasn't sure how at this point she was surprised as she walked in and peeled off her sweater – and yet somehow, she still was when it turned out to be the same temperature as the cold early-spring air that still hadn't begun to warm up for the year yet.

She couldn't wait for summer. She needed to thaw out at this point.

Moving inside the facility, she nodded her greeting to Grant and almost stopped mid-step when she caught sight of Matt standing in the middle of the floor, chatting to another blackbelt. He waved his greeting, finishing up what he was saying to his friend before sauntering over to where she had still not resumed walking.

"I thought you did BJJ…" she mused aloud, looking around as though she expected to see others from the same sort of class finishing up. There was no one familiar from that class, though, and as he stood there in a taekwondo uniform and not in the uniform she was used to seeing him in, she knew she was going to be subjected to the full hour with him. With a sigh, she accepted her fate.

"A person can't do both?" he questioned with a grin.

"Not what I mean... just didn't expect to find you here," she backtracked, hoping she could find a way that didn't sound like she was unhappy to see him.

"So you were avoiding me?" he joked, mocking offense as he held his hand over his collarbone like he was clutching at imaginary pearls.

She couldn't help the half-smile that pulled at her lips, her whole body already feeling lighter in the wake of her argument with Kai... and yet at the notion that any other guy could make her feel better, she crumpled.

"After all I did for you!"

For a moment, she watched his attempts to make her feel better, grateful, but she knew he could see the discomfort she wished she could hide, felt the change in him as his concern brushed up against her emotional awareness, warm and soft like a comforting bath.

Her lips dropped into a grimace as she fought to try and lift her own spirits. Guy or not, she had found a new friend in Matt, someone who understood the world she was living in in a way that Lucy never could and Kai was too close to – he had biases as her boyfriend, which meant he couldn't give her the outside opinion in her world she needed.

"You're incredibly sour for someone who's one step closer to having her mom home," he whispered as they watched the room around them, Matt leaning up against the wall beside her.

"It's nothing," she said, not sure she could rationalize talking to him about arguments that were just hers and Kai's.

"Come on," Matt pushed, bumping his shoulder with hers as she joined him leaning against the wall, her shoulders sagging as she sighed deeply. "What's wrong?

It's clear something is bothering you. And I know we're newly acquainted as friends but you know you can talk to me, right?"

She really looked at him, no ulterior motive clear in his face or aura other than the friendly concern she could feel. And she caved to her desire to tell him. "It's just…Kai and I got into a fight…" she started, watching his reaction as the knowledge dawned on him, testing out to see how he'd react.

He nodded slowly, his face not showing any hint of judgment as his eyebrows lifted only slightly in question. "Trouble in paradise?"

"No…" she corrected quickly before considering how to exactly phrase what had happened. "I just… He pointed some things out that I didn't want to hear."

"Oh?"

"We were debating the morality of torture," she whispered, glancing around at the room to make sure no one else was listening, and she heard the 'ahhh' as his face opened in surprise. It wasn't total though, indicating he wasn't as shocked by the statement as she expected him to be.

"And I'm guessing you were pro."

"Well… yes. After what you asked me yesterday, I realized there isn't much I wouldn't do to get her back."

"And he disagreed with your methods."

It wasn't a question, but she nodded all the same. "Yes. He mentioned a couple of things about stooping to their level in the pursuit being wrong."

"I know where he's coming from."

Matt's comment drew a small gasp from Mackenzie as she turned her head sharply to watch him. "You do?"

"Well, if you were my girlfriend, I'd hate to see you take on that burden too."

Mackenzie couldn't help a different kind of heat that rose in her cheeks as she considered what it would even be like to be Matt's girlfriend. And then as quickly as she'd considered the idea she tossed it aside, feeling the twist of guilt in her stomach at even contemplating the thought. Kai was a great guy, regardless of the argument they'd had, and she knew she shouldn't play fantasy just because of a couple of difficult things. Brushing the thought aside with a shake of her head, she focused on the main point he was trying to make and followed that. "It's not a burden, it's my choice."

"It is a burden even if it's your choice. It's part of the sacrifice you make when you do what needs to be done though. But it's hard to watch people you love sacrifice and cross lines when you know you'd gladly do it, so they didn't have to."

"I guess that makes sense."

"Of course it does. I'm not *that* stupid," he said with another smile.

This time, Mackenzie returned it a bit more easily, right in time for Grant to shoulder his way through the other arrivals to them.

"You two need to stop chatting and start warming up already. Set a good example, Matt. Then afterwards, can you take her through some more of our combo maneuvers?" he said, giving commands like an expert drill sergeant before his entire being softened when he glanced back to Mackenzie with a big, warm smile. "It's good to have you back, Mac."

"Nice to be back, Grant," she said, returning his welcome, reminded of how deceptive his outer exterior sometimes could be. She waited for the moment he started to move away before she mumbled under her breath, "And I'm really ready to punch something."

The sound of Matt's soft chuckle greeted her ears as he moved past her, starting to run laps around the gym.

Without resistance, and an almost-smile on her face, she did the same, feeling her blood begin its quicker course through her body and her muscles wake up, already complaining from their last venture through martial arts.

It didn't take long before the soreness faded slightly, a

perfect reminder of the strength she'd gain each time she returned. Her muscles would be sore and ripped each time, and each time they would be repaired stronger than before, ready for the next challenge.

Just like her.

15: THE FRIENDSHIP PROPOSAL

Mackenzie lay with her back on the mats, staring up at the ceiling, wondering how it wasn't condensing with all the heat and sweat that had penetrated the cold of the room. She took deep breaths, one hand on her diaphragm, trying to feel the expansion to prove to herself she was actually filling her body with what it needed.

Swallowing harshly a couple of times, she tried to rid herself of the foul-tasting bile that had worked its way up her throat after her first attempt at a sparring session. Thank god the space had begun to clear of people.

She had worked her body so hard she had been sure she was going to vomit, so when Grant had called for dismissal, she had done her end-of-class bow with the rest of them and then sunk to the floor and stretched out on to her back.

Matt had walked over the top of her in view, chuckling to himself as he removed his saturated uniform jacket. He had spent the end of class sparring against another black belt who had worked him just as hard as he had pushed them, the result a lightning-quick flurry of punches, blocks, kicks and movements on the mats that had every white belt including herself watching with rapid heartbeats and an anxious anticipation. At times she'd even struggled to figure out who exactly had the upper hand.

Her breathing had finally started to slow in her place on the ground, her muscles starting to set in with a tenderness that told her she would feel even more sore tomorrow than she had the last time. Sitting up, the muscles in her abdomen complaining even as she used her hands for assistance, she noticed Matt and Grant deep in conversation, the last ones left in the gym.

Sighing, she put her feet under herself and stood, taking off the taekwondo uniform to reveal the gym leggings and singlet top she'd worn underneath. Rolling and shoving the uniform in her gym bag, she traded it for her favorite, forest-green sloppy joe, which she threw on despite her sweat-covered skin, knowing the moment she stepped outside into the dark street she would feel the freeze as it touched the wind. She slipped her shoes on and moved silently around the outside of the mats, beginning to catch the men's quiet conversation as she approached Grant from behind.

"Walking her home again, Matt? If I didn't know any better, I'd say you liked this girl!" Grant scoffed as his upper body leaned back and he watched Matt.

Grant's amused surprise brushed up against Mackenzie's emotional aura, met with a glimmer of guilt from Matt. Mackenzie stopped for a moment, breath catching, still not visible over Grant's shoulder as she moved up to them, unsure if Matt had spotted her approach yet – eager to hear his response to the soft accusation.

"And do you know better?" he asked, chuckling, his voice disguising most of the response in amusement – but Mackenzie could hear the real question in his words: *Is it that obvious?*

Grant completely ignored the subtextual conversation, jumping straight to advice mode – to Mackenzie's shock - as she stood behind them, mouth wide, unsure this was actually what she was hearing.

"Look after her, man. From what I've seen, she

deserves a protector, not a time-wasting prick who's only looking for sex," Grant said softly, clapping Matt on the shoulder – and it was at that moment that Mackenzie realized she refused to hear any more of this.

Stepping out from behind Grant's big, burly muscled body that overpowered her size in every way, she made her presence known. "*She* is not looking for anything! *She* wants her friend to walk her home so she feels safe and then her protector boyfriend can take over," Mackenzie said, the edge to her voice making it clear she'd heard it all.

Both men stiffened – Grant more than Matt – and reeled for how to save the situation.

Mackenzie caught Matt's eye as he grinned his approval of her comment, his gaze flickering between her and Grant. She could tell by the way the back of his cheeks fluctuated and the way his pressed-tight lips twitched occasionally, that he was trying not to laugh at the utterly bewildered, guilty expression on Grant's face.

"It's okay, Grant, you didn't know," she said, offering him an out. "Hey, maybe you've taught me well enough that I can protect myself on the walk home already."

It was a light-hearted joke, hiding the fact that the idea of walking home alone with the Arcana around still terrified her and caused her heart to skip dangerously.

"Not quite there *yet*, Mac, but we'll have you as a dangerous warrior soon," he said, taking the offered change in subject and smiling gratefully.

"Well then, I guess you still have a job for the time being." She laughed, turning back to Matt before nodding to the door – her signal she was ready to leave this conversation and the gym.

With a wave and mumbled thanks and farewell to Grant, both Mackenzie and Matt headed out into the cold, only marginally warming as spring finally began to set into the weather.

Turning off and heading towards the Common, streetlights and shop window lights paving the way home, she tried not to think about Grant's insinuation. She tried to think of something else to say, but her mind kept going back to the notion that Matt wanted anything more than friendship – she wasn't sure it was true but his small inkling of guilt when it had been brought up said that some part of him might have wanted to.

Could she really fault him for what he felt, even if he never acted on it? Was it even a problem if he never tried to address it? Was this something she was supposed to tell Kai about? People's emotions were supposed to be private and could you really judge someone for what they weren't sharing? Probably not.

Matt broke the silence that grew between them, like a tensioned rubber band, ready to snap. "Did you want to go for a drink?" he asked, pulling out of her mental musings.

She blinked for a moment to let his words sink in and check that she had heard him correctly. "What?" she still found herself asking.

"Not alcoholic, obviously but it just seemed like you could use a little bit more time away from home before you head back to the stress of your hostage situation."

She stopped still, her mind running as she thought about what was stressful at home, wondering if he was insinuating Kai was keeping her hostage in her own home. She kicked herself as the gravity hit her like a physical slap in the cold, her memory finally reminding her of the orange-haired Arcana member tied up in her basement.

Her mouth dropped open, and her stomach twisted guilty as she realized how quickly one session at the gym had reduced the burning desire to punch something until she was left with all her steam gone, forgetting all about the scene she'd left behind.

She still didn't move, blowing the air in her mouth out through puffed cheeks as she gripped the strap of her bag tightly, nails pressing into the coarse material deep enough to feel like at any second they might bend and snap. Her eyes dropped, staring at the ground as though she could see her whole afternoon replay before her eyes if she looked long enough, her mind running on a tangent to curse her for forgetting what was really important. *What has Kai found while I've been gone? Has he found anything at all? He would've called if he'd gotten the answers we wanted, right? Or would he consider it something that I could wait to find out once I came home and he saw that the anger was gone...*

"Maybe some food?" Matt continued in her silence, waiting for something to catch as an idea she'd be happy with. "Unless... you're really keen to go home and return to torturing people to the dismay of your boyfriend."

Mackenzie glanced up from the sidewalk, the spell of the ground and her spiraling brain once again broken as she met his gaze. As though her body were answering for her, her stomach growled loudly, and she knew Matt had heard it by the grin that spread across his face, pulling it into a juvenile look of 'I told you so' that she wanted to slap out of principle.

She also wanted to hit her body for giving her away when her instinct had been to say no. Instead, she asked the only thing her brain needed to know before continuing this interaction with the new man in her life. She needed to tick this off for herself before she tried learning anything else about him. "You do know that *this* is just a friendship, right?" she asked, the grin dropping from his face at her words.

For a moment, he seemed uncomfortable, a flash of hurt hitting her through her magical awareness, but as quickly as it appeared, it was replaced by a cool and collected understanding that made her feel safe and warm – like someone had turned the thermostat to a perfect room temperature and the boiler had finally kicked in from its initial cold blast. "I know." He said it simply, nodding quickly as he crossed his arms.

"Because I love Kai. Despite our arguments and

disagreements, I always will. And I'm loyal to him," Mackenzie pressed again, watching Matt nod the same as before, making her flush with worry that she might have been saying it to convince herself. She dropped her gaze, the stress-inducing thought train consuming her until he softened her fear with his explanation.

"I know, and your boyfriend also made that quite clear when he came and apologized for the uncomfortable scene the other day."

"He did what?"

"He just wanted me to know you were spoken for and off-limits," Matt continued, a slight smile responding to her shock as she went from open-mouthed, unsure how to process the information, to leaning her head back to the sky and groaning as though it would save her from this conversation.

When it became apparent that nothing was dropping from the sky to rescue her from her own embarrassment, she faced Matt again. "I might be spoken for but I can speak for myself. He should know that," she clarified, watching him backtrack to defend his friend, hands raising in protection as though her words were a physical attack that required minimal effort to defend – but also a gesture of surrender.

"I'm sure he knows you can. But we've also been friends for a few years and we can be pretty candid with each other sometimes. It's fine, the message was received is all I'm pointing out," he said, and she sighed, dropping the subject as she realized it didn't require any more conversation. Matt was right; the message had been delivered, anything extra was just reiteration that became condescending to his morality. "Besides, I don't go after other guys' girls."

His smile, teasing, softened the air between them and she leaned into it, joining in with the beginnings of a grin as they began walking again. "Because you're one of the "good guys"?" she teased back.

"No, because I like having all her attention. It makes

things much more interesting," he said slyly, staring out at the darkness proudly.

Mackenzie's stomach growled again and she sighed happily, resigning herself to the needs of her body. "Okay, I will take you up on food but only because otherwise I won't make it home without my stomach eating my body!" She laughed.

"Yeah, we have to be careful. Need to make sure you gain all those muscles to become the strongest warrior fighter," he added as he spied a diner for them to disappear into, her nod pointing the way.

16: THE EMPEROR'S REIGN

The street was utterly empty by the time Mackenzie and Matt had finished their meal and stepped back out into the street again. A number of establishments that had cast their light out to the road when they'd arrived had long since gone quiet as the trek to Mackenzie's home began.

The smell of the hot greasy food - chips, burgers and chicken - lingered though, making Mackenzie feel sick as her full stomach weighed her down, threatening to have her rolling home with her food baby as a pillow.

Matt led the way, somehow unfazed by the sheer amount of food he'd wolfed down, which would have put competitive eaters to shame.

"You go on without me! Save yourself!" She laughed breathily as she pressed a hand to her stomach, hoping to hold all the food in there that she'd so recklessly ordered and then guilty made sure she ate the entirety of.

Matt chuckled, looking back at her from his few steps ahead. "Come on, Mac!" He picked up his pace slightly and she begrudgingly, with as much groaning and moaning as possible, followed behind.

Both Mackenzie and Matt were laughing as easily as they had through dinner, content for a small moment to just forget about the events that would be upcoming and what the world expected of them, and just have fun.

They were joking and laughing as though they'd been friends for years, and at least for that moment, Mackenzie was thankful to have another friend who she could be herself with and feel safe around.

Matt's foot touched the grass of the Common as he moved to cut through the park. Mackenzie was just as eager to get home before the food in her belly made her surrender to lying on the ground.

Matt flew from her vision through the air, smashing against the nearest tree with a loud crash.

Mackenzie screamed, post-food nausea forgotten as she looked around for an answer.

Appearing from the darkness to her left was Amari, silent with fury.

Instinctively, Mackenzie reached out with her magic, wondering how the rage so clearly displayed on Amari's face hadn't forewarned her of the woman's arrival – but she hit a mental wall. *A shield.*

With a shiver, Mackenzie backed up her steps, imagining the sword in her hand and willing it into existence, feeling the cool metal of the hilt against her palm.

She turned her head quickly, looking for backup from Matt, but he still hadn't moved from the base of the tree. She resisted the urge to run and check his pulse, alert at the enemy that she didn't know enough about yet.

Mackenzie looked between Amari and Matt, her mind reeling through the kind of powers that could do that, coming up with multiple options – all of them scaring her.

"You and I need to have words," Amari hissed, the normal gentle lilting tone of her voice when she was pretending to be sweet lost to her anger.

"And why's that?" Mackenzie asked, lifting the sword into view, acting as though she knew how to hold it in any way that would do the right amount of damage. With how her muscles cried out at holding the weight, and how tired her magic already was from her long day, it was all for show. She hoped Amari didn't make her have to use it because she was sure, despite her extra training and the adrenaline pulsing through her quickly, she'd still lose.

"Because you have something of mine."

"I don't know what you're talking about," Mackenzie responded, making sure not to answer too quickly, feigning confusion and straightening slightly. "But you've clearly stopped pretending to be friendly, so I'm going to have to ask you to keep moving."

Amari stalked forward a number of steps, her face cold and still as she surveyed her opponent, closing the distance between them as Mackenzie fought the urge to start backing up or run away.

Her muscles tightened, crying out as she stiffly held the heavy sword at the ready for the moment Amari was close enough to attack.

"I'm not doing that because I need answers." Amari held no weapons as she stood straight, watching Mackenzie hold the sword like she knew Mackenzie didn't want to have to use it.

"Well, how about we trade?" Mackenzie tried, her voice shaking as she spoke. "You tell me what I need to know about my mother, and I'll tell you what you need to know."

Mackenzie heard the groan of Matt waking up from his place next to the tree and breath returned, releasing the tightness in her chest slightly as she realized he was alive and now conscious.

But as her gaze returned to watch Amari, her relief was short-lived, Amari's hand raising towards the tree.

Mackenzie didn't have to look to understand what was happening: Matt gurgled, choking.

Amari's gaze stayed fastened to hers, the cruel smile pulling her lips as she held him there. "No trade. You tell me what I want to know," she said slowly, every word dictated like a command of its own. Mackenzie's hope was punctured with every syllable. She was becoming increasingly sure she wouldn't make it out of this situation unscathed. "or he dies."

Mackenzie's heart paused, as though everything in her were trying to decide how to play this – whether she should tell the truth or feign innocence but play along and risk Matt's life at the expense of her mother's.

"What do you want to know?" she replied quickly, feeling her stomach twist sharply inside her.

The gurgling quieted as Amari's outstretched hand loosened slightly.

"Don't tell her anything, Mac!" Matt tried to yell through his hoarse windpipe, earning a glare from Amari.

Mackenzie considered running her through with the sword when she wasn't looking, but couldn't guarantee it could do the job quick enough to keep Matt from being collateral.

"Where is Lily?" Amari said as she turned back to Mackenzie, her glare pointed and her chilled smile gone.

Mackenzie widened her eyes, darting her eyes around as though she were looking for the answer in the air before returning to Amari's as she spoke. "What do you mean?"

"I mean, she's been kidnapped and you're the only one I know who'd want to do that."

"Why?" Mackenzie asked, figuring that sticking to questions was the best way to keep her off the true scent.

Amari's eyes narrowed, her head tilting to the side as Mackenzie waited for an answer, feigning absolute fear. Her arm muscles started to shake, and she let it show, figuring it all sat with her image of someone terrified that she was being blamed for something she had no idea about.

She couldn't sense any of Amari's emotions – couldn't tell if her story was being believed – but she just had to trust herself or else. She'd made the gamble to risk it and not give away the only plan and leverage she had, and now she had to back it.

"Because you're trying to find your mother. Maybe you figured having Lily would be leverage – but I'm here to tell you it's not, and it's only going to get you and everyone you love killed."

"If I had her as leverage… don't you think I would have told you, or sent a list of demands?" Mackenzie posed, hoping Amari wouldn't guess at her other motives for taking Lily.

Amari paused mid-way through opening her mouth, as though she were about to speak but thought better of it. Silence fell between them as Amari reached for something else to say.

Mackenzie took it as her chance to push her innocence. "Please, let him go," she begged Amari in a quiet, breaking voice, watching the woman's eyes dart to her friend at the tree and back. Mackenzie felt like she was the one being choked, her breathing barely making it into lungs as she tried desperately to gulp it down. Tears welled in her eyes. "Please."

Amari stepped closer again, pressing her body against the tip of Mackenzie's sword. Mackenzie struggled against the weakness in her arms, fighting to keep it pressed in the same place.

Amari was daring Mackenzie to take the shot, her arm still holding on to whatever force held Matt's neck just light enough to keep him conscious, but tight enough to keep him from coming to her aid.

She leaned closer as she whispered savagely so only Mackenzie could hear. "If I find out that you had anything to do with my girlfriend's disappearance, I will disembowel you and pin your organs to the wall around you, and then kill everyone you love while you watch. Including your mother."

Everything in Mackenzie turned to ice under her stare.

"I could do it without you being able to put up a fight, you know?" Amari continued in Mackenzie's silence. As if to prove a point, she flicked her head towards Matt by the tree, and Mackenzie followed her gaze.

She watched as Matt stood up straight, able to breath again, taking the opportunity while it lasted. Then he looked down at his right hand, a small elaborate dagger appearing in his palm, his fingers tightening around the hilt. Its metal glinted with the light from the street lamps around them that showed his movements all too clearly as he lifted it, displaying his other palm flat to the sky and drawing a long line with the tip of the blade in it. Blood spilled over the sides of the hand, dripping to the ground below.

Matt didn't even flinch.

Mackenzie cried out, dropping the sword and letting it disappear from existence before it touched the ground. She wanted to run to him, to grab his hand and pull it out from where it pressed into his palm cutting along it, but as she turned back to Amari to find out what was happening, the answer was in her face.

Amari's concentration on Matt and her outreached hand, fingers moving and tensing as Matt followed her will, explained everything Mackenzie didn't know she feared.

The tension of guilt in Mackenzie's stomach stopped, surging with the overwhelming churning of nausea, the dizziness of the realization making her sway on her feet. "*You're* the Emperor," she whispered.

It wasn't a question but Amari's gaze flashed to meet hers, clocking the fear and paleness Mackenzie knew was on her face. Amari let her smugness show, her lips tilting up at the ends. "You've been warned," she said quietly before dropping her hand and walking away towards the bar she worked at, leaving Mackenzie swaying in the stillness.

Mackenzie was aware of Matt walking up behind

her, finally out of Amari's spell as he pressed his hand into his black sweater, letting the material soak up the blood that hadn't yet begun to clot.

It was as though she'd forgotten how to move, not sure how to keep walking with what she now knew. The adrenaline didn't want to leave her body, everything in her shaking and buzzing with the knowledge that terrified her.

Matt used his unharmed hand, sliding it under her elbow and leading her to her house, saying nothing as he guided her to the front door.

She was turning numb, even though her body continued to feel the effects of her terror and when she finally made it inside, nothing calmed.

She didn't feel safe anymore.

At the sound of the front door shutting loudly behind them, Kai walked into the room, a triumphant beaming grin lighting up his face, disappearing the moment he saw the state of Mackenzie and Matt.

"What happened?" he asked, his eyes darting wildly.

"Amari…" she managed to choke out in a whisper, her breath catching as she fought to stay calm, finally coming out of her dazed stupor.

Kai grasped Mackenzie's shoulder, his eyes wide, searching every inch of her body for sign of injury before looking over at his friend and spotting the hand pressed firmly into his sweater.

"Do you have a first aid kit?" Matt asked, following Kai's direction as he pointed to the kitchen.

"Under the sink," Kai called out as Matt disappeared to the other room, before turning back to Mackenzie and pulling her in close to his chest, his arms wrapping around her.

It took a moment before she noted she should probably be hugging him back, her mind running with too many questions of what this newest development meant for their endeavor to get her mom back. She wrapped her arms around his waist, feeling her arm muscles complain at being lifted but kept them up all the same.

Matt returned to where they stood, embraced, wrapping his knuckles in gauze confidently as his face lost the initial paleness they'd both arrived with.

Mackenzie was yet to improve at all.

Withdrawing from the embrace, Kai took Mackenzie's hand and led her in the living area, seating her on the couch as he sat beside her, and Matt sat nearby.

"Are you two okay? What happened with Amari?" he asked the two of them, flicking his head to see who could provide the information first.

Mackenzie found herself speaking. "She stopped us on the way home after training and dinner… to ask us about Lily." She watched the scared realization dawn on his face – eyebrows raised, mouth slightly open and eyes watching her expressions carefully. "I said I didn't know anything, but then she threatened Matt."

"You didn't tell her…"

"No. Or I imagine we wouldn't be here alone, much less alive. She… took control of him and made him cut himself. She… Amari is… the Emperor bloodline."

"Amari's the one with blood control," he stated flatly as he followed the realization himself, Mackenzie nodding her confirmation as she shivered at the memory of Matt cutting himself.

"Fuck!" Kai swore under his breath as he looked down at the floor.

"We're fucked! Unless we get answers right now, Amari's going to keep coming for us and who's to say Lucy isn't next… or *you*…" Mackenzie said, her voice breaking as the tears she'd been holding back slipped from her. She was lucky she wasn't also vomiting on the carpet like her body threatened to.

"About that…" Kai said, breaking into her pity party, drawing her gaze back up to his.

Even Matt, in her periphery, perked up at his words as they both caught sight of the attempted cheering-up smile Kai offered her.

"What?"

"I know where your mom is…"

The words shut down everything else but the question that sat on the tip of her lips. Her heart restarted itself, kicking up a gear as the excitement injected in her system. "How did you…? Where…?" she stammered, unsure where to begin asking, needing to know it all now.

"I just kept asking her questions and eliminating things when she lied to me until I eventually got the answer, location-wise and then when I had the location, I threatened to bring you back in and she caved and gave me the requirements of getting in. It needs *her* power to open the door, or the Emperor's, but I think it will be easier to use Lily's power than Amari's."

"You know where she is?" Mackenzie asked, her lip trembling as tears filled her eyes and she searched Kai's face for any sign that she'd misunderstood.

"I do. I know how to get her and we're going to go and bring her home tomorrow," he said, pulling her in against his chest.

The relief that washed over her was undeniable and the sobs that racked her body released all of the tension her body had felt for years.

Finally it was time.

17: THE EMPRESS' TURNOVER

Mackenzie packed the last of her clothing from the closet into the suitcase she'd brought with her when she'd moved to Salem, pressing down the lid and zipping it shut with a sense of finality that made her feel lighter. She picked it up, sitting it on its wheels, and walked out of the doorway, past where Lucy leaned with a soft smile on her lips and down the hallway to the room that had once hosted her old crib. Now, a small queen bed with purple-and-white bedding took up a large portion of the small room, and Mackenzie slid her bag onto the floor next to it.

Lucy followed behind her, watching as her best friend moved her life into the same room as hers.

They caught each other's eyes as Mackenzie looked over her shoulder and couldn't help the childish grin that spread across both of their faces.

"I can't believe we're finally going to bring her home!" Mackenzie gushed, the excitement in her heart that today was the day too overpowering to ignore.

"I know! It's incredible! I can't wait to see Anne again!" Lucy responded, grinning right back at her. It was hard to believe for Mackenzie that they'd now be roommates in this house in Salem - a place she wasn't sure was ever going to feel as welcoming as it did right now.

"And I promise once I'm home, we can sort out new

sleeping arrangements that are more permanent. Maybe turn the basement into a bedroom of sorts, and I'll move down there with all the weapons and magical items. I just want to say how much I appreciate you, how much I've *always* appreciated you being there for me. You've been my sister for so long, and I'm not letting you go anywhere ever again. You meant too much to ever say goodbye."

"It's okay. We'll assess your mother's state when she comes home before any decisions are made," Lucy said slowly, but Mackenzie couldn't help hearing the bittersweet undertone to it: her mother was coming home, but Lucy wasn't sure there was room for her in this house once that all changed.

Mackenzie stood up from her bag, walked over to where Lucy stood in the doorway, and took both her hands in her own. She met Lucy's eyes with a soft smile. She could feel the edge of doubt in her best friend's emotional aura, that worry gnawing at her light like a ravenous mouse with cheese. "I mean it, Luce. There's a place for you here, there always will be. I'm so thankful to have you in my life and that's not going to change, I swear. Blood or chosen, you are always my sister. You always were and always will be. You know I love you!"

"Of course! And I love you too!" Lucy returned the smile, seeming to relax at her best friend's words, and pulled her in to embrace her.

Mackenzie's hands smoothed up and down her best friend's back, feeling her sink against her, both girls leaning into each other. As they leaned back, catching each other's gaze they spoke again, they leaned on opposite sides of the doorframe with soft gazes and voices.

"I'm a bit sad I can't come with you to rescue her from that prison."

"I know, so am I, but we need as few people breaking in as possible."

"I understand the reasons why, but it's still annoying.

Also, can we just absorb the fact that this organization has an entire underground prison, because that's nuts!" Mackenzie shook her head.

"Yeah, it's scary! But we're going to get her out. You and Matt need to hold down the fort here and return Lily while we're gone."

"I know the plan, but stay safe."

"I will," Mackenzie whispered, only relatively convinced of her own promise.

"KZ, be careful. I don't know what's likely to happen, if anything, but just be aware… Kai would do anything for you and, in turn, your mother. He knows she's the most important thing to you; don't let him do something stupid in the name of love. Because you know he would."

"I know. I won't let him. Plus, with how this is all organized, it should all go to plan without a hiccup."

"When do things ever follow the plan?" Lucy said with a soft sigh, her face pulling slowly into a frown as the worry crept back into her emotions, her head leaning back to rest on the wooden doorframe.

"Don't jinx it!" Mackenzie said quickly, relieved when a smile forced Lucy's frown away as she chuckled.

Kai called up from the bottom of the stairs for her; it was time.

With her best anxious, hopeful grin, Mackenzie pushed off from the doorframe and headed down the staircase to where Kai and Matt waited.

Lucy followed behind her but found her own place to stop and wait, watching from halfway down the stairs, leaning against the wall littered with the photographs of the family she'd get to see – well, at least half of them.

The backpack Mackenzie and Kai were taking sat at the bottom of the stairs, loaded with an outfit each in case they needed it – one for her, one for Kai, and one for her mother from the clothing she'd left behind – as well as a first aid kit. She wasn't sure of the state she'd find her mother in and thinking too much about it made her anxious with no end.

Matt smiled at her broadly as she looked up from the bag to the two men on her team against the Arcana.

"Okay, Matt. You're the protector! Don't let anything happen to Lucy or this house while we're gone, okay? And make sure you wait for my text or Kai's before you release Lily. We don't need the Arcana figuring out what we're up to preemptively."

"We've already established this, Mac. You need to trust us now, we've got this." He nodded his agreement with a sure smile. "Now, it's time to do your bit before you leave."

She nodded as well, looking down slowly at the gold cuffs that adorned her wrists with a deep, heaving breath. They all followed her gaze; she could feel the weight of it as she thought about what she was about to do.

She hadn't tried this since her panic when she'd taken Teo's powers, and while it was different because it was in the heat of the moment saving her own ass, she was now about to strip someone of what had been in their family for generations. She was magically removing a part of them. She didn't know how long Lily had been awakened, how old she'd been when she first experienced her powers, what she'd done with them or if any good had come out of it. But she also knew Lily's soul now... Her emotions were poisonous and self-serving, and Mackenzie knew she could give the powers of the Empress a better home than they currently had.

Pushing her shoulders back, she took the last few steps down the staircase and headed for the basement door, not quite sure she'd ever be ready for what came next.

"Did you want anyone to go with you?" Kai asked, making her turn her head back to where the rest of her backup waited if she needed it.

Her heart swelled for a moment, feeling grateful and

thankful for the help she'd been given by these people. "No, thank you. I can do it," she said with a reassuring smile, puffing her chest out proudly as she opened the basement door and headed down into the darkness on her own.

The stairs were dark again as she descended, the soft breathing of Lily filling the space until she turned the corner and saw her sitting in the same chair as before, a little weathered and tired, her arm bandaged up by Kai. Mackenzie pursued her lips as she stared at the damage she'd done, finally able to feel the guilt now that she wasn't desperate and devoid of hope.

She would never admit that to Kai though – he didn't need to be right *all* the time.

She reached forward and took the gag off Lily's mouth as muffled noises came from her attempting to speak through it.

"What was that?" Mackenzie pushed calmly as she felt through the emotional aura of Lily, feeling confusion but nothing aggressive or angry, just the normal cold air that she was fairly sure was Lily's main setting.

"I figured you'd be all the way to Boston by now," Lily said, a cruel smile of surprise across her face.

"I had a few things left to do first," Mackenzie said simply, not prepared to elaborate, curious to see what Lily would make of the whole situation.

"Before rescuing your mother? Can't imagine what!"

"It's okay, it's nothing you need to worry yourself with."

"Rude!" Lily snapped back in response, drawing a flash of frustration from Mackenzie as she rolled her eyes and retorted, "No, rude is your girlfriend impeding on my perfectly good night yesterday."

At her words, Lily stilled, eyes wide as she froze in surprise. A flash of fear crossed through her aura. "You saw Amari?"

"Why do you look so scared, Lily? Worried because of what I might have done?"

"What did you do?" Lily squeaked in response, but Mackenzie could only pity her as she watched. After watching how the Arcana had treated her, Mackenzie couldn't imagine they treated their own much better, and it seemed a horrid way to live, always assuming the worst in people and looking over one's shoulder.

She smiled softly at Lily, her ill will towards her disappearing – just a desire to do what needed to be done, that was all that remained in her. "I'm nothing like the people in the Major Arcana… I did nothing to her and you'll be back with her soon enough."

"What are you, an idiot?" Lily scoffed with a harsh laugh.

Mackenzie merely raised her eyebrows as she waited for whatever opinion Lily had about how she did things.

"She'll kill you once I'm home safe and sound, you know that right?"

"I'm hoping that once you're back, that's not the case. But that's something I'm willing to gamble on and deal with if I'm wrong," Mackenzie said softly, feeling the sureness in herself since her conversation with Kai previously on the topic. The notion of being killed by Amari seemed to be a threat for all it was worth; they'd decided that the Arcana couldn't afford to kill her until they found a way to take her powers.

Mackenzie's team believed that the Major Arcana wanted the Magician's power for themselves more than they wanted her dead, and until they got that, she would be alive. For now.

"So you're really just going to let me go? Or are you going to make me unlock your mom's prison first?" Lily questioned, the buzzing of disbelief reaching Mackenzie as Lucy's mouth opened as though expecting some caveat, some catch that meant she'd have to screw over her girlfriend or organization.

With a genuine smile, Mackenzie answered again. "You know, I did consider that. But trying to transport a hostage all the way to Boston without us getting caught by the authorities or you escaping seemed near impossible. So I found an alternative."

Lily's aura snapped to suspicion, murky and heavy.

Mackenzie pushed her sleeves up, drawing attention to the gold cuffs that hugged her wrists, their cold metal against her skin, a welcome refreshing reminder that they were there to protect and assist her. The tie to her family that had saved her life once before would help rid Lily of the Empress power she didn't deserve to have anymore.

Lily's eyes widened as though they might bug out of her skull, and a scream escaped her throat, blood-curling and intense.

Mackenzie stepped back, physically unnerved by her reaction to the bracelets. She acted quickly, shoving the gag back in Lucy's mouth and securing it tightly. It minimized most of the noise, but Lily's terror still surrounded her, her feelings yelling at Mackenzie so loud she wasn't sure how others didn't hear them telepathically too. Even as her physical response grew when she stepped closer and placed her hand on her, she didn't hesitate.

Lily's body shook violently, the chains on her chair sounding as though she were sitting through an earthquake and the screams she tried to make through the gag looked like they would snap her vocal cords if given the air to make their full volume. She looked about ready to choke on the gag so Mackenzie acted quickly, pushing her way into Lily's mind, feeling sick as she was surrounded by the unending fear and terror, searching for the hint of tiredness she could use.

The alarm had driven it deeper, but thankfully not enough that Mackenzie couldn't eventually find it, focusing on it quickly to prevent Lily injuring herself in her panic.

Lily fell asleep nearly instantly, her eyelids sliding shut before she'd even realized what was happening: the long blink, closing them once and not returning them to their wide-eyed state.

Her breathing slowed so quickly Mackenzie stood still, a moment of panic, worried she had stopped it entirely, only relaxing once she heard the very slow heavy breathing through Lily's nostrils.

Lily's head dropped backwards, falling back into an almost unnatural angle without a headrest to the back of the chair.

Mackenzie's eyes flinched, narrowing in sympathetic pain as she stared at Lily's unconscious body. Making sure not to leave her magic behind, Mackenzie withdrew her emotional awareness, containing it inside herself, acutely aware of where every tendril of her magical aura ended and where Lily began, keeping them separate. She shut her eyes, knowing she needed to have complete focus as she felt for the cold magic that wanted to destroy the magic in others. She felt all the ties like spiraling strings inside her, working together to make colorful strands, each serving a different purpose – the Magician's, the Fool's, and the cuffs.

As she focused on the bracelets, their power came alive like a living snake in her veins, compliant and willing to do what she asked of it.

Commanding the bracelets to take from Lily as she pressed her fingers against the unconscious woman's cheek, cupping her face, Mackenzie felt the responsive phantom pulling feeling through the tips of her fingers like they were a vampire drinking from their victim.

The moment the drain of magic began, Lily's body moved underneath her touch.

Mackenzie opened her eyes quickly, watching in panic as Lily's body seized uncontrollably, shaking and thrashing against the chains. She didn't know what to do other than continue, pushing to make sure that the transfer happened quicker – her only solace was that because Lucy was gagged and tied, hopefully any injury would be near impossible.

Lifting Lily's head using both her hands, she held it in

place, up away from the neck-breaking angle it had been in before, feeling the muscle spasms underneath as she gripped tightly, hoping it would end soon.

For a split second, the feeling under her fingers changed – a feeling as though she were touching the leathery flesh of a leaf instead of smooth skin.

But it disappeared before Mackenzie could give it much thought and with it, Lily's body calmed, sinking in defeat as it stilled and limpness set into her limbs again.

Mackenzie pressed one finger into Lily's neck, feeling the steady pulse of Lily's heart against the tip of her fingers, and with a deep sigh, she felt the relief take any extra weight off her. Letting Lily's head go slowly, she watched it slide forwards, Lily's chin finding her chest.

Quietly, with her head held high and proud, Mackenzie strode away and up the stairs, ready to take on the Arcana and anyone who stood in the way of getting her mother back.

18: THE TRAIN TO ANSWERS

The movement of the local train, ever so slightly rocking side to side, was a monotonous lull that calmed Mackenzie as she sat in its near-empty carriage. The safety and sameness of it all threatened to put her to sleep as she sat up with her forehead pressed against the window, absorbing what sunshine streamed through the glass, and her hand securely holding Kai's. He was warm and comforting, his own emotional aura ready and happy, no hint of doubt in his feelings whatsoever.

The local train moved further and further from Salem towards Boston, it's movements easy and carriage's clean, but Mackenzie struggled to pull her mind from her town.

Despite her easy breathing, the niggling of doubt and anxiety deep inside her was slowly growing louder, demanding to be heard. She'd left it alone, not giving it voice or air since their departure from the house, convinced it would die without attention, but as she relaxed, resting for the adventure that waited in Boston, she struggled to keep it down. The worry that she was being watched by the Arcana as she'd moved from her home to the train, and then on board, wasn't a legitimate concern she had to tackle; her neck hadn't prickled with the physical sensation. It was only a feeling that only seemed to be growing – paranoia.

Mackenzie tried to look back at the track they'd left

behind through the window, feeling the distance like a rubber band, ready to snap and hit her with the full weight of what she was now intending to do. But the rubber-band feeling also brought with it the sense that when it snapped, her whole world might come crashing down – and with all this, the realization that she thought of Salem as her home.

For years she'd considered Salem to be her parent's home, the place they'd met and fallen in love, and Oregon had been her home. She'd moved to discover more about them, hoping to feel closer to them through their old house.

Even once she'd moved, months of chaos and anxiety still had her believing that she was a temporary resident who was there to learn. It had never belonged to her. But now... it did.

She wasn't sure when exactly it had changed from being just somewhere she lived to her home, but she felt wrong leaving it, even temporarily. Even though she knew she'd be back, she was attached to the warm, welcoming town, even with the tarot underworld that threatened her way of life.

The anxiety in her gut started to wake Mackenzie up, creating a restlessness she didn't know how to sate. The hopeful mood that had begun this morning as she faced the idea of her mother coming home was threatening to come crashing down with the wrong line of questioning.

Her heel tapped lightly against the floor of the train, speed increasing as she tried to force all her energy into her foot, hoping it would dissipate. It only grew though, the dangerous thought looming over her, begging to be asked until it exploded out of her.

Flexing her fingers under Kai's hand, she drew his gaze, his sleepy zone-out disappearing as he caught sight of Mackenzie chewing her lip in worry.

"What's wrong?" Kai asked softly, his voice the epitome of calming as he bumped his shoulder lightly against hers.

"What if happiness isn't meant for me?" she asked, staring straight away towards the only others in the carriage with them, far enough away to be out of earshot if they spoke quietly enough. She didn't look at Kai, not wanting to see the pained worry pull at his face – it was bad enough she could feel it in his aura.

"And why would you say that?" he pushed, sitting forward slightly in his seat to try and catch her eyes.

She had to admit she was thankful he asked for her reasons and to hear what was rattling around perilously in her skull, threatening to knock down any happiness she had.

"Don't get me wrong," she said. "I'm really excited to have my mom coming home, but it's been so long without her. I just keep expecting that it's all a lie."

"Well, I can tell you Lily wasn't lying, if nothing else."

"Not what she said, just… all of this. I keep expecting something to go wrong, or someone to tell me this is all a dream and I'm still back in Oregon in my bed with Lucy trying to convince me to get up and out of it."

"It's not a dream, Kenzie," Kai reassured her, his thumb tracing the back of her hand lightly.

The gesture soothed her slightly, but the power of her questions fought back still, wanting to pull her back under the waves of anxiety and rob her of the oxygen of hope. "I know, but it doesn't stop this horrible feeling in my gut that something might go wrong. That any happiness is short-lived… That the other shoe is about to drop," she said, letting the fear out into the world.

"All happiness is short-lived." he responded quickly, drawing her surprised wide-eyed gaze to find the sincerity and understanding plainly written in his face. "It's what makes life precious. It's short but it comes and goes, it might leave you but it will return too. It's what helps us appreciate it when we have it. You need the full breadth of emotions. But you can't let it snuff out your

173

happiness early because you're fearing its departure. That only makes you unhappy and serves no productivity."

"I suppose so…" She sighed, feeling his optimistic warmth with her magic, so sure in his words that it slowed the fidgeting, beginning to squash the fear before it took over.

"You know you're allowed to admit that I'm right sometimes?" Kai asked, a teasing grin lighting up his face as he looked up at her through his eyelashes, like he should have glasses perched on the bridge of his nose, inspecting her.

"You're *probably* right?" she admitted, a hint of a smile playing with her lips.

"Good. Now, why don't you tell me what about this all scares you? And then after, you leave those fears on the train and focus on the task ahead so we can make sure it goes to plan. Okay?"

"Okay…" she whispered, preparing the list of questions that wanted to derail her confidence. "I'm scared of what state my mother will be in. What if there are guards in there that Lily didn't know about or tell us, what if Mom doesn't recognize me or like who I've become? What if this doesn't turn out like we expect it to?"

"What if it turns out *better* than expected?" he asked back, stopping her in her mental tracks.

Why does he always know how to play Devil's advocate so well with my insecure thoughts? she asked herself as she realized how well he'd stumped her anxious reeling. She considered his words, letting the silence between them grow for a moment, only broken as he continued to quell the rising tide.

"It's the gamble we take and considering how much of your life has been guided by your parents, I am absolutely certain she won't be disappointed by the woman you've become."

Mackenzie searched Kai's eyes for any sign that it

wasn't true, that he had any doubt about what he was saying, but she knew even before she looked that he wasn't lying to her about this. He never would.

"There's also the matter of Amari when we get home…" she started again, changing the subject to someone more concrete and real of a problem, if not immediate. She remembered Lily's words and surety that Mackenzie would be in trouble when she returned home or released Amari's girlfriend, so much so that Mackenzie had worried if she should hold on to Lily until she was sure her mother was home safe and sound – but Kai had convinced her to stick to the original plan of freeing Lily the moment they had her mother out of the facility and enroute home. Time would tell.

"Let's focus on getting your mother out of the Major Arcana's clutches and then we can figure out our next steps," Kai reiterated, pulling an inadvertent sigh from Mackenzie's throat.

"She's the Emperor bloodline, Kai. I think she's going to be a problem the moment we're home. I know blood control relies on previous contact with the person's blood to work, but that means at least in our group she can use Matt or myself. Though how she got ahold of his blood previously, both of us are stumped."

"That does mean Lucy and I are safe. And Amari won't ever be able to control me, so that should help put your mind at ease. Plus, once we have your mom, you can start working on that mental shield again, maybe that will help."

"I don't think her power penetrates through the mind, I think it's body-based. And what do you mean she can't control you?" Mackenzie said, her spine causing her to sit up straighter as she tilted her head to watch him intensely.

"I'm immune," he said slowly, letting the news sink in.

It only confused Mackenzie more. "But how? Why?"

"Her blood control can only be done on humans and

because of the way the Devil's powers work, the beast is always active. So technically I'm not 100% human and my blood is dirty *or something.* The point is she can't control me, not now or ever."

"And you've tested this?" she asked, her hand grasping his tighter as hope filled her. The notion that he couldn't be used as blackmail against her with blood control made the whole nervous idea a little less scary. Only Matt and Lucy now remained as possible targets, a much smaller group to protect.

"One of my ancestors did. It was in his journal."

"You know, it's really annoying we can't read each other's family journals." She sighed quietly as she sank back in her seat, imagining what it would be like to read each other's and have all the answers the other knew. With any luck, it would provide solutions they hadn't thought of before. She couldn't help cursing herself for not considering the thought earlier.

"I understand why it's like that though. It protects you from stealing another family's journal if you can't read it."

"Oh, I understand why. It still makes it annoying when we're on the same team and sharing information would be great to have us on the same page!" Mackenzie said, smiling as she considered that prospect.

He beamed in response as he caught the lift in her expression. "Well, how about when we go home, you and I sit down and read the journals of our families to each other. That way we're both on the same page and we can give each other bedtime stories!" He chuckled, waggling his eyebrows.

"You know, now that I share a room with Lucy, we're going to need to spend a lot more time at your place, right?" she said as she thought about what "bedtime" he was really talking about.

"You don't think Lucy would approve of us having fun in your shared room?" he said with a wicked grin, and Mackenzie couldn't help the burst of laughter at the insinuation.

"I think she would whoop your ass the second the thought began to occur to try!" She giggled, hearing him join in as she imagined Lucy trying to bitch slap Kai for trying to initiate anything in their shared room.

"Okay, fine. I'm terrified of her. We'll move the romantics to my place then!" he said as his laughter subsided. "If only to also protect your mother's ears from the ways I defile you when we're alone."

His words had meant to be teasing, and for a split second the insides of her curled delightfully at his words before the idea of her mother worrying about that took over.

"Defile me?" she questioned.

"Well, we're going to have to test out how that new power of yours might come in handy." Again, teasing as he jokingly waggled his eyebrows. "Might have to see if you can control my beanstalk."

"Oh my gosh!" she cried out, laughing once again the way he'd intended her to at his cringey comment, feeling his emotional aura revel in triumph as she laughed once again. "That was the worst thing you've ever said, I swear!"

"Challenge accepted!" he continued, making her gasp in amused surprise.

"No! That wasn't a challenge! Ahh!" she said loudly, drawing the gazes of the elderly couple on the other side of the carriage from them at their volume – but she didn't care as she laughed hard enough for tears to form in her eyes.

As the humor calmed and the jokes died off, she sank happily against Kai, her head leaning against him, her temples sinking perfectly against the bone of his shoulder.

"Thank you!" she whispered to him, feeling the weight of her anxiety from before disappear, replaced by an overwhelming tiredness that pulled her eyelids shut longer and longer with each blink. The conversation had been just what she needed to hear, the ear to hear her problems and words to soothe her mind and soul. With a heavy sigh, she let herself drift off to sleep.

***

Mackenzie woke, her shoulder being jostled softly. As she blinked her eyes open to the light, she was reminded that she was on a train and jolted upright quickly as she looked around, worried that they'd missed their stop.

"It's okay, I'm just waking you now because we're almost there," he said softly, his voice calming the speedy frenzy inside her as he pulled the backpack from where it lay at his feet to his lap.

Blinking and wiping her eyes clear of sleep, Mackenzie let her body wake up slowly as she watched the world slow down beside her window. "I slept the whole trip?"

"I didn't want to wake you, I know you haven't been sleeping well lately." He smiled. "Are you ready to go?"

"As ready as I'm going to be," she said, watching the train start to brake and pull up at the station they needed, following Kai as they headed down the aisle, out the door and onto the platform.

The smell was hard to identify but it was strong, reminding her of the smell of hot tar as she walked away from the train to the clear port air of the rest of Boston, leaving the station behind.

Kai led the way and the further they walked, the more her senses awakened and the adrenaline at her scenario jolted through her excitedly, removing any remaining tiredness she felt from the train. She hadn't ever explored Boston, so as she looked at the buildings around her, she was reminded of the promise she'd made to Lucy before the chaos of her situation in Salem had taken over: of spending weekends exploring the cities together, enjoying what they had to offer and discovering the hidden secrets that were yet to be discovered in the sprawling metropolis areas.

The color scheme of the buildings seemed to reflect those around Salem, a dark red brick with white trimmings and finishing that had been repainted and cleaned but were still historic in nature. Other buildings littered in between floor to ceiling glass screaming modernism and everything about the city around her somehow felt old and new all at once.

Then she'd moved to Salem and her whole world had been taken over by the drama and magical underworld around her. She'd turned more than her own life upside down in the process and despite the choices not being entirely hers, guilt chewed a hole in her stomach uncomfortably.

Staring around at the entirely new city so close to her new home that she hadn't ever dared to explore before, she nodded to herself, promising that one day soon she'd take time out of her chaotic life to make sure she explored. And next time, she'd take Lucy with her – and possibly Kai. They deserved at least that much of a break.

Mackenzie and Kai moved between the buildings, headed down the street as Kai led the way towards the Major Arcana entrance in Boston that housed the prison Lily had described.

As they finally stopped across the street from the beginnings of a park, Mackenzie looked at Kai curiously, her eyebrows raising in question as she wondered where the doorway was.

His finger gestured subtly across from them, towards a white structure inside the Boston Common, and Mackenzie tried to hold in the scoffing laughter that pressed against her lips as she stared at the white structure in the park area that looked so similar to the gazebo in the Salem Common.

"You've got to be kidding me," she whispered to the air.

19: THE HEIST OF THE FOOL

Mackenzie and Kai had waited in a diner across the road from the Common for a number of hours, stocking up on energy using coffee and snacks as they waited for the cover of night to fall, watching the park carefully, noticing very little activity around the structure in question and none that indicated a magical presence. The Arcana hadn't caught on to reinforcing this prison yet.

The closer they got to the ideal time to strike, the more confident Mackenzie felt about the whole plan, convincing herself with each hour that there weren't going to be any unwelcome surprises and that she could do this.

Once the darkness had fallen and the time drew near, they paid their bill and moved out to the park area. Sitting with most of their bodies out of sight of possible onlookers, Mackenzie sat behind the rock wall and pressed her hand to the grass, determined for the last hour before they headed closer to the gazebo-like structure to learn how to use Lily's power over nature. They had to ensure a smooth process to get inside and if the Empress's power needed to be used to do it, she had to make sure she had control.

The moment Mackenzie's hand touched the blades of grass and her body settled into the sense of relaxation, she felt the magic. Like ties were holding her to the earth that she could command, she could feel the welcome energy of the nature beneath her. It was like a balance of everything inside her, a dichotomy of peace and chaos, effort and instinct.

Working through it slowly, Mackenzie let her fingers weave between the blades of grass in the darkness, focusing on feeling the way her insides linked to the world around her. Slowly, she let herself branch out with the magic, testing its strength and capacity, unsure what to expect but also scared to take it too far with no written assistance.

With more time and planning, she would have had time to study her family journal and to learn the power, but it was time to collect her mother and there was no stopping her from doing what needed to be done. She focused on the blades of grass between her fingers, willing them to grow longer, making sure she only isolated it to the powers of the Empress – feeling the manifestation powers of the Magician wanting to comply but pushing them aside for the moment.

The green blades complied, pushing the limits of what she thought was possible in record speed, growing before her eyes. As it did though, she watched the grass around it begin to wither and die.

The gasp of surprise that escaped Kai's lips as he watched, though, told her he was just as surprised by her at the revelation.

"Seems like the balance I'm feeling is mimicked in the magic tool. I can't create without taking at the same time," she whispered into the dim light as she stared at the results of her magic, mesmerized.

"You'll have to be especially careful with those powers then, until you know more about the extent of it. But at least for the moment you seem to have a handle on how to access it, which is hopefully all we need to get inside."

She nodded, withdrawing her hand from the ground and watching her hold over the earth stay, not reversing even as she pulled her magic away. It appeared this magic was one that held permanently. Or at least, even after her magic effects no longer controlled it.

They didn't have to wait much longer for the crowds of the Common to file away, draining to the diners and bars around them, only the occasional late-night stroller wandering their way through the park – easily avoided.

Hand in hand, they got up from their place next to the wall and headed to the white structure that Kai had indicated before as the entrance.

Finally, the anxiety began to make Mackenzie fidget. She stretched the fingers of her unheld hand continuously, flicking them as though they were coated in water she couldn't feel, and her heart started to tap rhythms to her in morse code she'd never heard before.

When the base of the structure finally stood before them, Mackenzie considered praying to whatever god or entity had given her powers to let this go smoothly.

"It was here?" she checked with Kai, lifting her head to look at the monumental stone structure that put the Salem gazebo to shame. At its base was a door, seeming to be for storage of some kind. Mackenzie stood in front of it, reaching for the handle. The moment it connected with the metal of the door, she felt a burn against her skin, like the handle had been super-heated.

Hissing and flinching, she retracted her hand quickly, letting go of Kai's to nurse her injured hand by the wrist, checking for a burn mark on her palm.

Nothing was there and as she stared at the uninjured bit of skin, she heard the large *thunk* from the door in front of her, like a great heavy lock had been slid away from its holder. She snapped her eyes up, feeling Kai standing directly over her shoulder do the same and they both watched as the large metal door down the steps under the stone structure swung open.

For a moment they both stood there, Mackenzie feeling the same dumbstruck emotion in Kai's aura as she imagined was etched in her own face.

Time was of the essence, but she could barely believe that was it. A mere fake injury from a door handle to unlock the entrance and she was able to explore an underground tarot-family facility?

Shaking it off, Mackenzie led the way, descending ever-so-slowly into a darkness that robbed her of all sight.

Kai was behind her, she could hear him breathing in the space around them that, despite not being able to see, she could tell was close to her body. It was claustrophobic even without the use of light, and step by step, she moved further down in the pitch black, relying only on her ability to feel out where the next step ended.

Eventually, in her slowness, making sure she didn't take a tumble down the stairs with a wrong move, Kai caught up to her. It was good to know he was there as she moved down, his body so close he was beginning to press up against her with each step, his hand brushing her arm to reassure her, available to grab and catch her should she fall.

Her hand found a railing to the right, cold, – iron by the feel of it, guiding her even further in the never-ending darkness.

Eventually, as though she'd stepped through some sort of blackout veil, light appeared in the distance down the stairs. Soft and dim at first, red like a fire, her steps picking up speed the closer she got to it and the more she could see of the steps below her. The confidence had her nearly running, feet shuffling step to step at record speeds until she came to the bottom of the staircase and the source of the light.

Wooden torches, scorching with a steady fire, sat on either side of the tunnel walls, close enough that she could smell the smoke when they flickered. She looked ahead down the passageway that turned into a close tunnel, dirt the whole way through, and pulled the torch off the wall beside her with all the force she could muster. The iron holding it to the wall gave way, clattering to the floor, the torch releasing from its frame.

"Subtlety isn't your strong suit, is it?" Kai said quietly as the noise of the frame hitting the floor rattled off the walls ahead, echoing back to them.

She showed her teeth, gritting a smile before beginning to move again.

There was no time to lose and she took off, only holding herself back from running due to the many rocks that protruded from the dirt dangerously, threatening to have her wiping out and falling onto the hot torch.

She didn't hesitate in her steps until the space broke outwards into a cavernous room with three doors, one of which was already opened and unlocked. She stood a moment, considering if she should try the other doors, but followed her gut that urged her just to keep moving.

She ran into the very left doorway and nearly hit her face into a rock wall ten steps in. She halted in front of it, searching the edges for a sign that the wall was temporary. With one hand outstretched, she patted it down, smacking her hand restlessly against the stone wall that blocked her path, testing it and only serving to scrape skin off in her frustration. She grunted, looking back over her shoulder to see Kai's amused face, watching her from outside the doorway in bewilderment.

"What?" she snapped at him, not having the time to figure out why he thought she was so funny.

"You ran right past it…" he replied, looking at something near him but just out of sight for her.

Stalking back to the cavernous room, feeling her gut heat at the delay in finding her mother, she caught sight of what Kai was referring to. Two pedestals lay before the three doorways, and on them were gardening pots. As she moved closer, with her torch illuminating them, she noticed in one pot was a glorious orchid, thriving down in the cave room despite the lack of sunlight. And the other appeared to be empty, but on closer observation, she realized the corpse of a dead orchid lay in its soil, dried and browned so it almost camouflaged. Kai's gaze trained on a symbol engraved into the clay of each pot, nodding as he seemed to understand its meaning.

"The unicursal hexagram," he said softly, all amusement gone on his face as it scrunched in thought.

"The uni-what-now?" she echoed, eyebrows nearly knitting into one as she stared at him like he'd spoken another language. The term meant nothing to her.

"Magic symbol. It represents unity and balance," he explained, only slightly sating the bouncy, itching desire to speed up her progress.

She didn't like any delay, though, and even though she was beginning to piece together how to keep moving, it wasn't quick enough.

Shoving the fiery torch in Kai's direction, she relinquished her control over the light and instead put her hands out, one in each pot, the dark soil cool between her fingers, her palm resting on the surface as she focused inwards to concentrate. She knew the balance, especially with the powers she'd required to enter, and now was the time to find the mental balance again within herself.

It was harder this time to calm her mind and let her body find a balance between impatience and patience, calm and frenzied, considering how close they stood to freeing her mother, but all the same she pushed herself to do so.

Feeling the pull through her own body, she shut her eyelids slightly, trying not to stare at the closed doorways, feeling the visual of them pull her emotions radically towards impatience and desperation.

Breathing deeply, eyes shut, trying to force the current situation from her mind, Mackenzie waited, feeling the tiny changes around her fingers, the grounding of the earth below and above and around her. She tried to imagine the perfectly balanced see-saw in her mind. Tried to image the dead orchid regrowing to half the life it had had and in turn, taking the amazing growth from the flourishing orchid.

The click of the locked door told her she'd done it and as her eyes snapped open, she retracted her hands from the soil in the pots quickly, looking for a moment in astonishment at what she'd left behind. The dead flower was very much alive, revived in its pot to be a sickly looking orchid in dire need of water, and the vibrant flower to her left that had been brighter and more alive than she'd ever seen a flower was much the same as the first. She wasn't sure whether to be happy or sad about reviving one flower and slowly killing another, but she ignored it all the moment her eyes caught on the open middle doorway ahead that had previously been closed and shut.

She broke into a run, ignoring the torch and Kai, feeling him recover to follow behind her, his steps echoing off the tunnel walls to remind her of his presence as she steadily increased her pace, sprinting by the time anything changed in view.

She scooted to a halt, almost running straight into the back of the person that stood in front of her. *A guard.*

According to all Lily's information, he was the only one that oversaw this prison and he was the only other person they'd have to deal with before her mother.

Wide-eyed and frozen in place, it took a moment of them assessing each other for anyone to act.

He launched into motion, reaching for her, his other hand reaching for a holstered gun while Mackenzie hurriedly launched into his emotional aura, feeling like she was diving in a pool of freezing cold water she had not been prepared for.

It didn't take long to search the guard's emotions and feelings to find the tiredness in him – everyone had it somewhere – but staying down in a dark and dank cave wouldn't have made him feel lively in the least. Mackenzie pulled that viciously into focus for him.

His fingers wrapped around the hilt of the gun,

tightening as Mackenzie watched warily before they released and he crashed to the ground.

With a second to take a deep breath and sigh her relief, Mackenzie looked up at what lay behind the guard.

Kai moved up behind her, his pace slowing as he realized she'd stopped, concern flashing only for a moment as he clocked the unconscious body that lay at her feet before his gaze tracked hers and they stared horrified at what lay before them.

The prison was one long corridor Mackenzie couldn't see the end of. Each side of the corridor was a cage with bars separating the cold metal that ran the full way down the corridor, the walkway through the middle. The only light in the room came from the torch Kai still held – and one more at the close end of the room, next to where the guard had been standing.

Yanking that off the wall also, Mackenzie moved over to one side of the walkway, peering into the first cell.

Tired, weak eyes peered back at her, drawn by the light and noise, the body of a person who had been kept here for some time, clothing dirtied and sullied, a foul-stench reaching her from inside that she feared to know the source of. She looked back at Kai, who moved to the opposite side of the walkway, doing the same, checking the first cage he found.

Mackenzie reached her magical awareness out ever so slightly, keeling over as the feelings around her bombarded her senses. She fought to keep the torch away from her face or from dropping the only light source the room possessed, almost burning her face in the process. Pain, misery and sorrow overwhelmed her, hollowing out everything in her, robbing her of breath. Inhaling through a scrapy throat, feeling the pressure against her head, all Mackenzie wanted to do was scream, convinced doing so would relieve the pressure.

As she opened her mouth, a warm hand pressed on

the back of her shoulder, lifting her upper body up and away from the fire she leaned too close to, pressing her back against the warm presence of Kai's front.

"Hey, it's hard. I know. But you can do this," he said quietly, so much that she almost didn't hear him over the inordinate amount of psychic emotional noise consuming her thoughts. "Focus on me, only me. Don't go far out, pinpoint on me."

"I can't…" she gasped as tears glassed her eyes over and robbed her of sight, turning her mind into a watery den of horror. She'd never known pain – or utter hopelessness – like what they were feeling and she didn't know how to escape it. "It's… I can't pull away from it, Kai."

"You have to or we're not going to find her, Kenz," he said, his words reaching deep inside her to find that pearl hidden beneath the murky waters of her stomach and finding the one thing that could push her through and remind her of how to keep going.

Her mother was one of these voices, somewhere amongst all of the trapped souls in these cages. She needed to rescue her.

Mackenzie nodded once, trying to pull her body up from where she'd sunk against Kai's body, feeling her legs shake slightly at the motion.

"Do you remember what she looks like?" she whispered as she walked closer to the cages, finding Kai's soft concern in amongst the sea of anguish and focusing on it like she would an emotion in an aura, finding her magic comply and tune out the others. They didn't completely disappear, the other emotions still weighing her down like a physical heaviness on her shoulder, but as she pushed her mind to Kai's, she hyper-focused on him. She wanted to know the moment he had any human recognition, so that she knew before his words were even uttered that he'd found her.

"I've seen those pictures on the wall enough, you just focus on looking," he said assuredly, and without any further hesitation, Mackenzie and Kai began to incrementally work their ways from cell to cell, peering in with the help of their torches to look through the prisoners.

Mackenzie didn't know what any of these people had done, whether they deserved to be here or if they had just gotten in the way of the Arcana, but she fought every instinct inside her that said she needed to unlock every single cell she passed. That could end badly and hinder her from finding her mother, so for now, she held.

Mackenzie's steps gathered speed as each cell she passed turned up people who were most definitely not her mother, the tears that had been in her eyes sliding down her cheeks, unrestrained as she met the eyes of people who looked at her like she was there to save them from this hell. The smell only grew worse the further in they went, no part of her becoming used to the bombardment of her nose.

She didn't want to become used to it, though. She wanted to feel every part of this once she had her mother, to know what the Arcana had left these people to. The fate they had no doubt received without trial or fair judgment, just for whatever they had done to the Arcana or what they had not given them. The dark rage built from her chest out, heating her in a way that lit a fire, blazing and determined to break free if she let it.

At the same time though, her outer exterior was crumpling in fear. As she finally found the end to the long line of prison cells, she realized the person she hadn't found yet.

Glancing over her shoulder, she saw Kai having the same success rate at finding her family as she was. Her fingers shook as they tried desperately to hold on to the fire torch, her hands sweaty despite the immense cold that hung in the space outside the proximity of her light.

With only five cells left, she checked them quickly.

With each one her entire body threatened to shut down, to unleash the pain she was now feeling as rage at the Arcana.

Two cells remaining, and one was empty.

At the last cell she hesitated, unsure what to do. It held an elderly woman, near her eighties. How she'd survived this long in the cells, Mackenzie had no idea. The graying hair and soft eyes shone in the light of the torch but all that she saw in the old woman's face was pity.

Mackenzie's eyes didn't dare leave the elderly woman's – didn't dare voice aloud what she was scared to admit to herself – feeling the lump in her throat creep up higher, trying to choke the air from her windpipe.

She stood like that for a time and the old woman didn't break her gaze, as though she knew Mackenzie just needed a place to focus so she didn't see the lack of cells and the plain stone wall that now sat to her side, signaling the end of the prison.

Kai stopped behind her, the aura she had been so tuned to only emanating a worry, strong and wary, and a dismay that didn't even begin to measure against Mackenzie's.

20: THE FURY OF THE WITCH

"She's not here," Mackenzie whispered, her gaze not leaving the old woman's, still trained to the eyes that stared at her with such pity – as though she knew…

"Kenz, I'm so sorry. She –" Kai started, only to be cut off by Mackenzie whipping around to face him, her body daringly close to his as she held the fire torch, wide-eyed and shaking as she shook her head frantically, her dark red ringlets trying to escape her ponytail.

"She's got to be here! She's here! I know it!" she said loudly as though by sheer volume alone she could overpower any other opinion.

His lips pressed together tightly for a moment, and she could see his disbelief, and she refused to hear it.

"Kenz…" he said slowly, searching for the words as she stared at him, her head still involuntarily shaking side to side as she tried to convince him not to voice it. He was wrong, and she couldn't hear the words come from his mouth.

"*No*! She *has* to be here! You would have known if Lily had lied to you and she didn't, so she's got to be here somewhere!"

"Kenzie, I don't thi-" he tried again, but she fought harder and harder to figure out where her mother could be, entertaining no possibility that involved her not being here.

"There's an illusionist in the Arcana! Someone who makes you see things differently than they are! What if

she's here but she's been disguised? She could be…
What if it's just an illusion we're seeing?"

She could see him begin to open his mouth,
speechless to find the words as she felt the sharp pain in
his aura. Before he could say anything more to her, she
headed down the side of cells Kai had checked, back the
way they'd come much more quickly than she had
before, yelling for answers.

"Anne! Anne? Anne!" she called again and again,
hearing it echo off the caved walls around the cells,
feeling it reverberate from the metal bars.

The faces that looked up at her as she shoved the fire
close to the bars shied away from the sudden light, none
seeming to recognize the name.

The panic around her in the bodies of the cells grew
though, some that she passed climbing up to the bars
behind her and beginning to yell also. It was nonsensical
pleas for help or just trying to call her back to let them
out, only serving to drown her voice out as she
continued to yell for her mother.

As she reached the entryway, Mackenzie turned and
went back to where Kai still stood in the darkness, going
back past the faces she'd seen the first time.

No one answered in recognition.

"Anne! Mom? Mom, please be here! *Anne*!" she
screeched, everything about her shaking and weakening
the closer to the end she got again.

She noticed Kai hadn't tried to follow her, and as she
finally returned to where he'd stayed standing, she could
see the way his eyes watered as he looked at her.

Her own streamed down her cheeks, so much
flowing that they were no longer singular tears anymore
as she wiped them away uselessly, only to be replaced by
new rivers before she'd even finished ridding herself of
them.

His mouth twisted as though he were going to say the
words that finally let her broken heart shatter, and all
she could do was stand there, lowering the torch and

letting it drop to the damp floor, shaking her head.

"Don't… Please don't say it," she whispered out in the darkness, watching the light in Kai's hands illuminate the glassiness of his eyes with all the tears that threatened to fall from his eyes.

"Kenzie… I don't think your mom's here," he said, his own voice cracking a part inside her as she heard the phlegm on the back of his throat.

"She has to be. She's probably just somewhere else here. There's got to be another room with more cells."

"This is the only prison the Major Arcana has," he said softly, his eyes lowering from hers as she felt the pain in his aura at his own words.

"They're a *secret* organization. They're probably hiding any others."

"Kenz, I checked. They aren't any more."

"No!" she screamed finally, not wanting him to say another word.

He didn't try, watching and staring at her in silence as she tried to come to her own conclusions, afraid to come to the same one as him.

"Mackenzie?" a voice whispered from behind her, making her turn. The old woman from before watched her, head tilted to the side in curiosity, and as Mackenzie probed her emotions, she sensed wonder and disbelief, but no recognition or love. It wasn't her mother in disguise.

"Do I know you?" she said, peering closer at the woman, expecting to recognize something in her face.

Her face was worn and tired and scuffed with dirt and dried blood. The clothing she wore looked like it had been worn for years, torn in places and hanging off a frame that had shrunk out of the initial size the clothing was intended for. The shirt hung like a cloak on her when the style of the original would've hung nicely, accentuating curves. Not any more.

"You don't. But you are Anne's daughter, aren't you?" she asked, moving up to the bars of the cell.

Mackenzie looked the foreign woman up and down and despite the shape she was in and the bars she stood behind, Mackenzie crossed her arms and tried to stay skeptical, not wanting to believe this woman might have known her mother. She wasn't sure what angle this woman had to play. "Of course I am, why else would I be calling for her? Do you know her?"

"I did," she said, her eyes filling with the same pity from before as she spoke.

The two words in past tense made Mackenzie's veins cold, like ice water had been thrown on the back of her neck and she was forced to keep still through it all. "Where is she?" Mackenzie asked quietly, the sounds of the other prisoner's yelling tuning out as she focused on the old woman's lips as she spoke, trying not to show how the words held her captive as she waited to hear the fate of her mother.

"You won't find her."

"Why not?"

"A young woman with dark skin and eyes and a cruel smile came here, and was ready to use her as bait to control you. She was bragging about it."

Mackenzie's eyebrows lifted at the mention of Amari, and hope blossomed in her chest. *She'd been taken as leverage.*

"Your mother didn't like that."

"Where did they take her?"

"They didn't."

"What?" The warm hope squashed quickly, and everything in her stilled as she waited for anything that told her she could keep on being optimistic for her mother's sake.

"You won't find her here, or anywhere, for that matter. When she found out the kind of power her life held over you, the things they talked about making you do in the name of saving her, she killed herself."

Mackenzie sank to her knees, letting the stone crack into her kneecaps as she fell, uncaring of the flash of pain it caused. She barely felt it.

"She refused to be a bargaining chip anymore."

"When?" Mackenzie asked the ground.

The old woman's croaky tired voice answered. "A few months ago. I'm sorry, sweetie, you didn't miss her by much."

A scream unleashed from Mackenzie's throat, guttural and wrenching, as though she could fling every bit of pain in that moment through the Earth and blast her way out of the prison by agony alone.

The world around her responded with a deafening crash, echoing her pain for all to see.

21: THE STORM OF THE WITCH

Mackenzie didn't remember how she got out of the Major Arcana's prison. Before she had realized what had happened, she was in a nice hotel, Kai beside her, leading her through the door of a room he'd checked them into.

In a daze, she walked inside, spotting the beige colored walls, the mixed textures and the white pristine bed sheets that looked too perfect. The white seamlessness of the made bed broke through her numbness and as she stared at it, head cocked to the side, all she wanted to do was ruin it. Rip the sheets apart and splatter it with oil and foods and anything that would stain its covers.

Nothing can be that perfect. It's all fake, she growled in her mind as she watched it with a murderous stare.

Kai let her elbow go for a moment, leaving her to muse on the best way to attack the bed. He dropped the backpack by the bedside table, drawing her gaze. He looked so tired, worn out and heavy, like the weight of the whole night rested only on his shoulders.

She wanted to feel bad for him, wanted to run to his side and comfort him, but the energy to do so wouldn't find her. Not after tonight.

It was hard to ignore the reality now looking her in the face. Hard to run away from the words the old woman had said to her before she'd let the entire prison feel her pain.

The prison cages blowing open their locks, releasing

their occupants… Watching them escape in desperation, trampling the guard to death in the process. She'd watched it all, uncaring for his life as she curled up on the stone floor, letting the sobs overtake her.

She'd wanted to keep crying on the ground of the cave prison, but eventually she'd run out of tears and at some point Kai had gotten her out of there. The rest was a lost memory.

And now here she stood, with nothing left to cry and no more emotions she wanted to feel. She willed time to rewind back to before she'd been given false hope about her mother. When she was dead and missing. Before this hope had created an elation in her that had only sought to tear everything in her to shreds when it was smashed.

Everything was cold, and nothing felt right.

Kai walked into her sight, drawing her gaze again as he approached her slowly, like she might explode at any moment. His hands raised in defense, he took step after step until he stood in front of her, pulling her into his chest.

It took a moment to realize he was shaking just as much as her, his body holding back sobs and his emotional aura pressing against hers, gutted by sadness. "I'm so sorry, Kenz. I wish we could have saved her," he whispered against the top of her hair.

She shut her eyes, willing herself not to cry again.

His hand stroked up and down along her spine, sniffling as he squeezed her closer, as though he were trying to push the liquid from her eyes. "We never should've gone."

She didn't say anything, worried she couldn't trust her own voice. She didn't want to move, didn't want to escape the only safe place left in the world for her. She didn't want to go home or face the world again, or the Arcana, or even Lucy. How could she tell Lucy what had happened, that she wasn't coming home with her mother?

They stood for a time, and she could feel her legs

wanting to release her to the floor, sinking her body weight against Kai.

He swayed, staring at the bed longingly for a moment as though all he wanted to do was get in it and not climb out. She agreed with the notion. Instead, he leaned back and looked her up and down, spotting the dirt-covered clothing she wore and had pressed onto him in the hug, and sighed.

Taking her hand carefully, lacing his fingers slowly with hers, he walked her to the bathroom. The same as the bedroom, the white in this room was pristine, the tiles too bright amidst a world she only wanted to ignore.

Kai turned the water on, letting the room fill with steam as it heated, and caught Mackenzie squinting in the bright light, reflecting on the white tiles glaringly. Without another thought, he turned on the round makeup mirror light and switched the overhead LED off, turning the bathroom to a dark room, dim yellow lighting highlighting the edges of their silhouettes.

Mackenzie stood there dumbfounded as he held his hand to her cheek softly, pressing his forehead to hers. She sighed against him, the tears she thought she didn't have anymore leaking down her cheeks in the darkness one by one.

Pressing a kiss to her forehead, he slowly took the ends of her shirt, lifting it up.

She complied, holding her hands above her head as he leaned back and pulled the shirt over her head, leaving her torso exposed except for the tight bra she'd worn that felt more like a chest noose than a practical support device now.

Kai pulled his own shirt off quickly, letting them stand watching each other in the dim lighting, and he pressed himself closer for a moment, reaching around and unclasping her bra.

She reveled in his skin on hers, the safety of his warmth heating her, and leaned in to his shoulder with her forehead.

He waited a moment, hugging her again before moving once more, slowly removing himself from under her weight as he continued to undress her.

Unbuttoning her pants and sliding them and her panties off, she stepped out carefully, waiting for him to instruct her on what to do next, no longer feeling the energy to choose anything anymore.

He pulled his clothes off, and she prepared for him to warm her body and console her with sex, but it never came. Instead, he led her into the large shower cubicle, shutting the door behind the two of them, and pulled her close as he embraced her under the hot water. There was no condition to his touch, just safety, just… being there.

"I know it hurts right now," he said, his voice loud in the tiled room despite his quiet tone. "You'll make it through this, love. You always have and you always will. You are the strongest person I have ever met and it kills me that the world has not rewarded you for it. I hate that you have had to prove yourself again and again."

Her body shook, the beat of her broken heart rattling her every time it dared to move. She didn't say anything, she couldn't. She didn't know how to speak or say the words she wanted to say. Voicing her thoughts would not do them justice – or would break her entirely. She buried her face further into his chest, unsure which was the water or her tears anymore as she felt his hands hold her steady.

Eventually he leaned back, taking the bar of soap from behind her, unwrapping it and sliding it along her skin. It was tender at first, harder in the places he found the dirt caked but never painful.

It wasn't like she would've noticed anyway; her tolerance for it had become so high, she was sure that short of splitting her skin open, she wouldn't feel anything.

"You're going to be okay eventually," he kept

whispering as he leant away from her and sank to his knees in front of her, his face in line with her stomach. His hands guiding the soap worked gently on her kneecaps, scuffed and bleeding from her collision with the ground earlier in the night, scooping around her legs, collecting and removing the dirt and watching it wash down the drain.

He looked up at her from where he knelt, and through the water-logged eyes she stared back at him. She didn't know how to give him a reassuring smile or tell him that he was the only reason she thought she'd be able to go on in that moment. Her lips scrunched as the tears built stronger than before and she slipped her hands to his head, her nails scratching his head lightly, feeling him lean in to her touch.

Even without the help of emotional powers, he seemed to understand what she wanted to say, pressing his face into her stomach heavily.

"I love you," she whispered, her voice breaking as she tried to think of anything else to say – to no avail.

"I love you too, Kenz. Always. If I could find some way to save you from this pain, I'd do it in a heartbeat."

"I know," she said, barely audible against the sounds of the water.

They stayed that way, letting the water shift down the drain, making its noises, swallowing up the room in its everyday sounds until they felt their extremities prune and Mackenzie began to sway.

She needed to lie in the bed with Kai, and never get out.

Sensing the change in her, he rose, switching the water off and instantly letting the cold of the outside world creep back into their space. He pulled a towel from outside the shower, reaching out of the booth and leaving the door open to a place she barely wanted to visit. He patted her down only slightly before he wrapped it around her shoulders and scooped one arm under her knees, the other behind her back.

Lifting up, ignoring the water that dripped from him as he moved, he carried her out of the bathroom carefully. Setting her on her feet for a moment, checking she was stable and not swaying dangerously before moving, he reached into the backpack by their feet in search of extra clothing.

She could tell he was trying really hard not to pull it all out, aware of the third set of clothing in there; she wasn't sure how she'd react seeing the outfit her mother was going to wear home. The one she'd spent a painstaking amount of time choosing with Lucy, even though now it seemed silly.

Any clothing would have been better than the soiled stuff they'd made the prisoners in there wear. Choosing the perfect outfit for her mother to come home in was a luxury she wouldn't have cared for and Mackenzie now knew was futile.

Kai pulled Mackenzie's clothing out carefully, not disturbing any of the other items in the bag enough to knock them out. Placing the clothes on the bed, he lifted the shirt up, shifting so that Mackenzie would be able to let it slip over her head easily without assistance. It looked like a prison to her, it looked like acceptance to going back to her life without her mother and she didn't want to.

She could feel the pull of magnetism from the squishy, pristine-white bed behind her, calling into its depths. A place to escape into that she never planned to leave. A warmth. A safety.

Before Kai could even hold the shirt out, prepared to help wrestle her into its restricting cloth, Mackenzie pulled the sheets back behind her and – with the towel still wrapped around her – she climbed into the bed. She sank into the mattress, feeling its softness claim her despite the water droplets that still littered her skin. As she sank the duvet over the top of her, the combination of towel and blankets created a warmth that lulled her, welcomed her, held her in a heat that calmed her nervous system and heart.

Kai turned for a moment, watching her as he let the shirt drop. With his half-open mouth, he looked like he wanted to argue with her and tell her she couldn't cave to the calls of the bed in her state, understanding her history with it.

But her eyelids drooped, the amount of magic she'd used weighing her body down heavily into the mattress as the tiredness took over. With a yawn, she watched the decision of Kai to say something to her disappear.

He moved off to sit at the desk in the entry hall, switching the bedroom lights off as he went.

Sleep claimed her quickly but didn't hold her tightly enough. Mackenzie dozed, waking up in doses, not sure how much time had passed before she was pulled under by the heavy soul again. The blackout curtains had been shut, not telling the secrets of the time outside the room.

Kai never joined her but didn't force her up at any point either; she woke a few times to his fingers stroking the flyaway strands of hair off her face but he was always otherwise sitting at the desk, his head in his hands as he propped up on his elbows, massaging his temples with the ends of his fingers as he stared at the dark timber between him and his lower body. It didn't look comfortable, but in the same way that he left her to escape to the depths of her subconscious in sleep, she let him tackle his mental thought demons and whatever they spoke to him.

The ring of a cell, speedily cut off by being answered in the main entry hall, broke the half-asleep daze she was in.

"I texted you saying we were alive and that you could let her go. What else do you need?" Kai said quietly with a sigh as he answered the phone to – what she could only assume was – Lucy. He waited, listening to the voice on the other end of the phone that Mackenzie knew she had no chance of hearing.

"She's not with us," he continued, his tone dropping

as he began pacing the entry hall, his silhouette hunched over as he held the phone to his ear and leaned into it quietly. Mackenzie could tell he was being careful not to wake her. "I'm sorry, Lucy. She was already gone when we got there."

His steps slowed and he stood still in view, waiting.

"Well… apparently Lily wasn't aware of the fact that Anne had taken her own life a few months ago to save her daughter from being controlled… I know… She's not in a good way. She broke open an entire prison with her power when she found out. I… haven't seen *anything* like it. I'm not even sure if it was the Magician's power that did it or… something else."

Silence ensued as he waited, beginning to silently pace again, his socks sliding against the timber flooring to minimize the noises.

"I don't know what else it would be! Just that it's ridiculously powerful whatever it is. I don't know *what* we released on the streets either, but it can't be good… Yes, the power smashed open all of the cells in the prison, everyone got out before I could even realize what was happening and… they killed the guard on the way out."

He sighed as whatever was said on the other end of the phone sank in, leaning against the wall, facing Mackenzie in the dim light so she could see how tired his face was, how he stared at the floor as though it could give him the answers he didn't currently have. "Nothing went to plan."

More silence.

"She's resting at the moment," he said simply, flicking his eyes up to her.

She caught his gaze, giving him a sad smile where she sank into the pillow, trying to reassure him with her face, but she wasn't doing a good job. She could feel by how weighed-down her under-eyes were that she probably looked as tired as him.

"You can release Lily now, I think. Just be careful

when you do."

He smiled back at her, pushing off the wall slightly as though he would move to her side, but his steps froze in their tracks at whatever had been said over the phone.

Mackenzie's heart lurched at the stillness on his face, the utter attention he paid the words, his eyes not seeing her anymore.

"What do you mean something is wrong? She.... Why would she... And you already let her go?" Kai echoed, trying to wrap his head around Lucy's words.

Mackenzie sat up, ignoring the fact that she was still naked, the towel well and truly lost in the depths of the blankets.

"Oh fuck, are you sure? *Fuck!*"

Mackenzie threw the blankets back and bounded off the bed towards Kai, ignoring clothes and blankets and modesty as she stopped directly in front of him, drawing his gaze up at her as he hung up on Lucy, looking as though he wanted to throw his phone at the wall.

"What is it?" she asked, feeling her heart speed.

"When Lily lost her powers, she lost her memory of the Arcana."

"What?! But I was careful! I didn't touch her with the Fool magic. I made sure of it!"

"It would appear that's the price paid for losing your magic."

Mackenzie's stomach dropped as she thought of the ramifications of what she'd done to Lily, what she'd robbed from another person – and how this news would affect Amari, who wouldn't really be getting her girlfriend back.

Looking at Kai, she knew exactly what he would do to the people that dared erase Mackenzie's memory. *Fuck.*

22: THE EMPEROR'S REVENGE

Nothing made Mackenzie more nervous than when Lucy stopped answering her phone. Usually it indicated that her best friend was giving her the silent treatment, letting her stew in order to feel bad about whatever it was Lucy had deemed wrong.

It seemed less likely this time that Lucy had something to be mad about; she might have been mad at Mackenzie after letting the prisoners go in her emotional outburst but it was less likely.

It was even less so when Matt stopped answering his phone too.

The train couldn't move fast enough towards Salem as Mackenzie stood, hands braced against the back of the seat in front of her, unable to keep herself still.

Kai watched her, his own foot tapping as he tried not to broadcast his own anxiety to her, seeming to forget the way his emotional aura brushed up against hers because of how in tune they were.

The bad, sick feeling in her stomach didn't settle the closer they got to Salem as she desperately sent text after text to Lucy and Matt, begging for any response. Nothing came.

With each unanswered message and call, the feeling only seemed to grow inside her.

Second by second ticked by, but all Mackenzie could do was wait, trying to think of a faster way she could get off the train and arrive at home.

As they drew nearer to the station, and the horrid

feeling in her stomach continued, she tried to soothe her nerves by placing the gold cuffs on her wrists underneath her long-sleeved shirt, no longer sure what to expect. Scared to find out the answer.

She knew she had to set her grief aside. It would always come second to the lives of the people she cared about and right now, that was in question. She couldn't break apart, or lose her mind. She had to stay level-headed and keep her focus on her magic. For Matt. *For Lucy.*

Finally, the train slowed into the station and the moment the doors let her off, she was bounding down the platform, running for home.

Kai was just as hurried, catching her quickly as they both sprinted down the main street.

Her feet didn't move fast enough as she soared across the roads, hearing the traffic complain about her impulsive choices with the sounds of their horns.

Kai kept up with her perfectly, getting ahead slightly, only to tilt his head and realize and sink back to stay in line with her.

"No," she said, through her heaving breaths in her sprint. "Go ahead. Don't wait for me. They're... in trouble. *Go!*"

As though her words commanded him, and realizing how much he was holding back, she watched Kai take off ahead. His animalistic powers let him shoot his way forward, and it didn't take long before he disappeared so far ahead that she lost sight of him.

She cut across the Common, no hesitation in her steps as she bolted over the grass, nearly tripping on clumpy sections multiple times. But with each stumble, she recovered and kept going until she hit her front porch.

The door lay wide open and she couldn't help hoping that it hadn't been found like that by Kai. But as she slowed in the doorway, glancing around frantically, she didn't have the time to ask him. Shivers danced up and down her spine like they were having a late night orgy and her insides felt like they were being removed by an ice-cream scoop..

The room was empty. The living area was empty, as was the kitchen, and as she strained to hear, very little noise reached her ears beyond the usual house sounds.

And then she spotted it.

The moment she realized the basement door was ajar, she took off again, her steps mimicking the rapid beat of her heart as it tried to fight to stay behind in the entrance hall – not prepared to see what was down the staircase.

The further down she got into her basement, the louder the voices became, she cursed as she realized whose voices.

Amari. Kai.

And as she rounded the corner, she spotted Lucy and Matt tied to metal chairs, restrained by chains the same way Mackenzie had done to Lily, and gagged. Their eyes widened as she came into view and saw the rest of the scene. Kai was in front of her, facing Amari, who had taken one of the gold adorned spears off the wall, its tip dripping with fresh blood.

Frantic, Mackenzie found the source of it on a gash across the shin of Lucy's leg.

Fury burned in her gut, her eyes burning daggers at Amari as she stood up next to Kai, ready to cross the distance and return the pain to Amari.

"Get out of here," Kai growled quietly under his breath, drawing Mackenzie's laser gaze.

"No way! Not until they're safe," she whispered back through gritted teeth, barely able to believe the request had left his lips.

"With her power, you won't be able to do anything. She could have you finished in under a minute just with a thought!"

"I'm not going *anywhere* without them!"

"Kenz, I can do this. You'll be a distraction. Get out."

"No."

"May I interrupt this lover's spat?" Amari screeched over their voices, and both their heads turned sharply to the noise as she stood, the spear tip pressing against Matt's jugular. "Considering you took mine from me."

Mackenzie stammered, trying to figure out what she could say. "I didn't…" she started, but the look on Amari's face as she pressed the spear deeper into Matt's neck made Mackenzie gasp tightly, afraid his skin would split under the point with how hard Amari pressed.

"Don't lie to me," Amari spat and Mackenzie's mouth flapped open, trying to find any words in her anger and shock to stop Amari.

"I didn't know, I swear!" she managed, watching Amari's face twist up angrily.

"Didn't know you were kidnapping my girlfriend or didn't know she'd lose her memory?" Amari asked again, as though she was looking for confirmation that Mackenzie had in fact done it. "I know you took her powers, you're the only one with the artifact to do it!"

"I didn't know that she would lose her memory. I only knew I needed the powers to get in the prison to find my mother, and I couldn't take her with us to Boston," Mackenzie said, choosing truth, knowing it didn't really matter to keep it secret now that she'd lost what she wanted from the venture.

Amari's face lightened, a cruel smile gracing her lips as she watched Mackenzie in amusement, the spear not moving from its place.

Mackenzie tried to consider how to stop her if she decided to take his life, how she could save him from the spear, coming up blank as she tried to find something to conjure or a way into Amari's mind before she could press just that little bit harder.

"Well that was a useless venture then, wasn't it?" Amari laughed, and the emptiness in Mackenzie's body seemed to be filled with ice.

"You knew?" she whispered, eyes wide as she

watched Amari in horror.

"Of course I knew! Who do you think watched her do it?" She snickered, and Mackenzie realized the absolute lack of humanity in Amari; there was no reason to feel bad for what she'd done. Lily and Amari had been an incredible match, perfectly compatible in their cruelty – but the world didn't deserve the two of them together, that was too much.

"If only you'd told Lily…" Mackenzie mused aloud, and the laugh dropped off from her face like it had been slapped off. Mackenzie kept drilling the Emperor, enjoying the way her words tortured her in return, enjoying the revenge from what the Arcana had driven her mother to. "I *never* would've taken the powers if I realized there was nothing for me in Boston. If Lily had known my mother was already dead, she wouldn't have told us what *she* thought was the truth and sent us there looking for my family! You did this to her, not me! You didn't tell her the truth and now she's gone and she's forgotten about you. You can try to blame me all you want, but I was doing exactly what you should've expected when you shoved that knife in my gut and told me she was alive. Was it a lie then? Or did you ever plan on returning her to me?"

She stepped closer to Amari, watching her hand holding the spear shake only slightly – in rage or utter horror she didn't know but Mackenzie took it as her chance. She approached slowly, knowing her Fool powers would be no good so long as Amari could block her out, so instead she'd have to go back to the original: the Magician.

She kept her gaze on Amari but envisioned in her mind's eye the same spear floating in space behind the Emperor, focusing on forming it with a tip just as sharp as the one that now drew blood from Matt's neck. She wouldn't have much time, and she was thankful Kai stayed vigilant and alert where he was, waiting for her to make her move. She had to be sure the clone spear was ready; she only had one chance to strike and make sure she halted any further action from Amari. "You had to know the moment I knew she was alive I would be coming to her rescue, and after what you drove her to, watching as she did it, I will make sure you feel every bit of pain she did. That will be my retribution."

"Retribution? Such a big word for such a good girl. Are you sure you have it in you to try?" Amari asked, slowly recovering from the temporary shock of Mackenzie's words, her cruel amusement returning and the strength in her limbs revitalizing. "Because I did make you a promise the other night that I plan on delivering. Do you remember?"

"Every word," Mackenzie said confidently.

"And?"

"And that might be a bit difficult," Mackenzie spat, pulling the spear as hard as possible through Amari's back, watching as it protruded from the other side, splashing blood against her light blue shirt.

The way Amari's mouth opened as though she were going to scream, only to cough up blood, was an image that would haunt Mackenzie for years to come. The feeling of hot liquid splashing across her face, as she realized what it was, made Mackenzie want to vomit. The bile rose quickly in response in her throat and she fought hard to swallow it.

The spear in Amari's hand clattered to the floor as her hands instead clasped around the metal of the spear that pierced her body. She dropped to her knees, blood still leaking from her mouth as she gaped at Mackenzie.

Mackenzie rushed to the closest chair, and began frantically undoing the chains that held Matt to the chair, checking his neck injury as she did so, thankful it wasn't deep. At the same time, she was thankful Kai acted just as quickly, doing the same for Lucy.

Once the two were free, they were helped up from their chairs quickly, Mackenzie and Kai intending to help them flee the situation.

"Okay, now you get out of here with these two!" Kai commanded quickly, and once again Mackenzie was turning her nose up.

"I'm not leaving you! And which one of us just skewered her, you *need* my help!"

"I can do more with you not around."

Lucy gasped in pain as she put her weight on her injured leg, still bleeding, the gash the spear had left looking like it might need stitches soon, or at the very least, a medic.

Mackenzie grabbed the backpack off Kai's shoulders, thankful when he followed her logic quickly and shrugged it off and handed it to Matt.

"Get her out of here now! Take her to the Order!" she ordered, watching him nod without hesitation and swing one of Lucy's arms over his shoulders, helping take the weight off her injured leg.

Then he moved as quickly as he could, surprisingly so considering the hissing she heard from Lucy's lips, back to the basement stairs and up them, telling her over and over to just push through for a moment until they were out of there.

Mackenzie turned back to Amari, Kai following her glance also to see the woman rising, seemingly using her powers to conquer the pain the spear had to be causing her. She looked beyond rage and the hairs on Mackenzie's skin stood on end. Instinctively, she made sure to check the tie with the spear, not letting the magic disappear, but the moment Amari's eyes lifted to hers, she knew she was in trouble.

"Fuck you!" Amari grunted, and Mackenzie dropped to her knees.

She wasn't sure how she'd ended up there but next thing she knew the air left her lungs. She began clawing at her throat, trying to remind her body how to breathe – to no avail.

Her vision darkened quickly. And the magic slipped from her grasp, causing the force that held her to only

211

get stronger.

She heard Kai scream in rage, and then the world lightened and the breath returned.

She glanced up to see him rolling with Amari, who tried to throw punches in her close quarters but did very little damage, unable to get the wind-up required for any real impact.

"You have to trust me too, Kenz," he yelled as she struggled to her feet, watching the fight closely.

One of his arms shifted quickly into his beast form, pressing the clawed paw down on Amari's throat as he managed to get her upper body flat.

She batted at the paw and what she could reach of him uselessly, spasming under his body.

Mackenzie almost smiled, but his words had hit something in her and she knew he'd made a point. This had all been a clear example that she could still be controlled, and he had the upper hand and would remain to do so because he couldn't. She'd spent so long worried he didn't trust her, but she needed to make sure he knew she trusted him too. And she did.

She turned quickly, running for the basement stairs and focusing on building the mental wall up like Kai had taught her.

She knew the moment the walls couldn't be erected fully that something had gone horribly wrong, that she was in more trouble than she knew how to handle and that she should have acted when Kai had first told her to.

I should have left sooner, she cursed as her body halted of its own accord. She could recognize exactly what was happening, think and worry about it and try to tell her body to do something else, but it was futile. It was like she was not in the driver's seat of her body anymore.

She ought to feel the rate of her heart panicking, frantically banging its way to be free but she was inside her own mind as her body turned back to Kai and

Amari, and it stayed calmingly quiet.

Heart rate steady, her nerves untensed, and the utter lack of sensation threw her. She met her controller's gaze, only able to move her eyeballs the way she wanted to.

Despite the paw that still squashed Amari's throat, her head was turned slightly, watching her with a cruel smile pulling up at the sides of her lips as she noted how the magic worked despite her attacker's advantage.

Mackenzie could feel the sensation of the magic moving through her body, listening to demands that weren't hers, and it was like she was screaming out as loud as she could. The only magic she could sense was the Fool's powers, which were useless against Amari as she conjured a knife in Mackenzie's hand.

Amari made Mackenzie look down at it, made her watch as the ornate knife – an exact replica of the one that had stabbed her in the gut months ago – appeared in her palm. She wanted to scream, surprised when her mouth began to comply to her demands, opening to let the sound free.

Her eyes lifted to Amari, whose sadistic grin had only grown. That small flicker of hope that she was regaining any modicum of control faded as quickly as it appeared, dashed at the realization that she'd *allowed* Mackenzie this ounce of freedom.

Shutting her mouth, Mackenzie saw that Kai still hadn't spotted what was unfolding.

Maybe this is her last ditch effort because he's about to knock her out, she thought. She'd prefer to wait than endanger him by yelling and giving Amari the upper hand at his surprise.

Swallowing the scream, she pressed her lips tightly shut and didn't let her controller have the satisfaction of hearing her horror.

Amari wouldn't let him stay ignorant though, her eyes returning to Kai's face, sneering.

"Get. *Back*," she forced out with the last bits of breath

she had in her lungs. Her gaze flicked to where Mackenzie stood frozen, unable to move, holding the knife.

Kai's head whipped around, finally aware that something was wrong, that Mackenzie hadn't managed to escape in time. He didn't hesitate as he moved off Amari and to Mackenzie's side.

The knife lifted at his approach, her hand guiding it until the blade edge sat across the front of her throat, pressing sharply. Mackenzie's eye flinched as Amari let her show the fear she clearly wanted to see.

Her controller coughed a couple of times, keeping her eyes skating back and forth between the two of them.

"I'm sorry. I tried to leave…" Mackenzie said to Kai. Her voice cut off as her hand pressed tighter against her throat, the sudden movement silencing her. Her eyes frantically switched from Kai to Amari, feeling as though she should be in tears – terrified for her life – but nothing came. The rest of her body didn't react. "I *do* trust you."

The knife pressed harder and she could feel the pain spreading around her neck, sharp and aggressive.

Kai's eyes widened, watching her as warmth drifted down her neck, dripping and spreading its heat slowly all the way down her chest.

"I made you a promise, Mackenzie. And now I'm going to keep it," Amari said viciously, her smile sliding off her face and turning into a rage-filled scowl, standing up and stepping closer to Mackenzie. "Kai, get on your knees now or I cut deeper. Hands behind your back."

He complied, dropping where he stood silently to his knees beside Mackenzie, merely a foot between them.

She wanted to reach out, to pull him back up and tell him to kick Amari's ass, but she knew it was useless. As Lucy had pointed out to her, he wouldn't put Mackenzie's life at risk.

But Mackenzie didn't believe for a second that Amari would keep her safe in all this – she knew Amari had promised her a death after watching everyone she loved die and she was unable to stop it. Kai was her only chance, unable to be controlled except by the notion of saving Mackenzie.

"Kai, save yourself. Get out of here. She'll kill you," Mackenzie choked out before her lips were shut for her, and she caught the hardening features of Amari who'd clearly had enough.

"It's okay, Mackenzie. I know how to save you," Kai whispered as he stayed kneeling beside her, making Amari scoff as she moved to grab the chains from the chairs.

If Kai let his wrists be chained behind his back, like Amari clearly planned, this was over. He would die and she would have to watch, and then so would she.

Her body was tight, holding the knife in place and no matter how much she thrashed against the magic that held her, it was no use.

Amari's eyes left the two of them for a second, reaching down as part of the chain slipped from her grasp, attempting to regain it.

Kai acted quickly. He grabbed Mackenzie's free hand and she felt his warm presence, confused by the act. "I love you," he whispered as a surge of power overcame her.

The stronger it got, the more she felt Amari's hold on her disappear.

The panic realization dawned on her as her heart rate kicked up.

"No! Kai, you can't! Please stop!" she screamed, still unable to pull away but feeling control over her mouth return.

He gritted his teeth, holding on to her hand tighter, the feeling in her fingers trying to pull away from him. "Let go!"

The bracelets felt like ice, but they weren't listening

215

to her, pumping Kai's powers into her body. The cuffs on her wrists that she'd forgotten she was wearing were fulfilling their purpose, their sentience knowing nothing different than what they were designed for; she was the wearer and he was gladly donating his powers to the owner.

She screamed louder, control of her body now wholly back in her hands. One hand dropped the knife, letting it and her magic disappear from the equation.

Her focus remained as she leaned her weight away from Kai, fighting to pull her hand from his grasp, crying in frustration as she did. "Kai, please. Don't leave me," she shrieked, meeting his gaze.

Even through his tight, gritted expression, his eyes met hers with confidence, working hard to hide the pain that was hitting him. His aura didn't lie though, and she knew the moment his powers disappeared and she'd failed, because it all snapped to black.

Kai's eyes rolled back in his head, shutting, and his body slumped to the ground.

23: THE TURN OF THE EMPEROR

Kai's body went limp as his eyes rolled back in his head and then shut. And then he went tumbling towards the concrete flooring, his face primed to smack into the ground face-first.

Mackenzie launched forward, dropping and catching him by his shoulders, holding him from the impact, lowering him slowly to the floor on his back, surprised at how serene his face looked when unconscious.

A rage awakened in her gut, the fear entirely gone as she felt the creature in her stir. It only made it worse at the reminder of what she'd just gained – and what she'd lost to collect it.

The anger wasn't at the unconscious person at her feet as she stood though. Turning back to Amari, she spun just in time to see her, chain still in hand, running at Mackenzie.

Mackenzie planted her feet and let the weight shift properly as she threw a punch, connecting with the bottom of Amari's nose.

Pain lanced up her arm as her knuckles made contact, the skin breaking on impact. She fought not to cry out, pulling her hand back to nurse it as she did so. It was nothing like punching the padded shield at martial arts class she'd become used to lately. She cupped her injured hand into her chest, discouraged from punching again as she followed Amari's faltering backward steps.

Holding her bleeding nose, Amari's eyes flashed with

icy rage Mackenzie hadn't seen in her before. The face that had once been friendly, serene and beautiful to her housed no loveliness anymore.

Remembering Matt's words during class, Mackenzie didn't let her have the space or time to regroup, chasing her down to continue her attack. Determined not to lose her less-dominant hand to split knuckles also, she flicked her leg out in a kick, driving the ball of her foot into Amari's stomach.

Grunting, Amari bent over Mackenzie's leg pressed into her body, spitting out some of the nose blood that had made its way into her mouth from the back of her throat. Mackenzie moved forward, working to keep the upper hand, letting her own anger drive from deep in her stomach, a vicious creature hiding under her skin, wanting to be free.

Amari whipped her head up, tracking Mackenzie's approach, and swung the heavy thick chain at her, forcing her to dodge.

Despite her attempt, the chain connected with Mackenzie's neck, swinging around tightly once before losing momentum on the second side and landing heavily down the center of her back, knocking the air from her lungs in surprise. The chain wasn't tight enough to rob her of the ability to breathe but it did make it harder.

Amari yanked the chain from where she still held it, pulling Mackenzie's weight forward by her neck.

The ground moved towards her and it was only by stumbling and trying to be quick on her feet that she recovered enough as she neared Amari to take her to the ground like Matt had taught her in BJJ. Straining to remember the lessons at speed, she was thankful for the drilling, her body automatically working to pin Amari before she had been able to recall all the instructions.

As Amari fought to free herself, her arms and legs slowly losing the ability to move in the position Mackenzie had shifted them to, her eyes widened.

Something dark in Mackenzie reveled at the fear she saw flash across Amari's face.

"You are the reason for all of this," Mackenzie hissed in Amari's face with all the venom and anger she could feel inside her, staring at the woman who had caused so much of her pain for the last few months. So much of her fear, her paranoia, and now it stopped. She refused to let the Arcana rob her of anything *ever* again.

"It was worth it. You took Lily from me. It's not how I expected you to lose yours, but it's only fair!" Amari responded, just as much anger in her.

Her words shocked Mackenzie; how anyone could think everything Amari had done to her was fair was utterly warped. "Fair? You took my mother from me, used her as a source to control me when I began to question the Arcana, and watched her die for me in front of your eyes and did *nothing*! And you have the audacity to talk to me about stealing Lily from you? I have nearly lost everything in my life because of you and your fucked-up organization!" she screamed.

Amari worked not to flinch puffing her bottom lip out in proud defiance, looking as righteous as ever.

Before Mackenzie could question her choices or think about if she'd regret it, she manifested the same knife that had stabbed her in the gut months ago and shoved it into Amari's side.

A breathy cry escaped Amari's lips and a small crack appeared in her mental wall, the flash of pain reaching Mackenzie from Amari's emotions.

Before it could disappear, Mackenzie latched onto the emotion, following it through the small gap and leading herself into Amari's aura. She knew what to do, wading her way through the rage, pain, and sorrow that tried to boil Mackenzie out of her head. She pushed on, determined, finding the tiredness in her aura, prevalent with the pain that radiated through her aura as well.

Working quickly, Mackenzie pushed it larger, making sure it hit Amari fast, in the same way she had with Lily.

The moment Amari's eyes shut, Mackenzie focused on the bracelets, cold and powerful and hungry, and let them steal again. She didn't care about the way Amari's body jolted jarringly underneath her and that blood leaked out on the concrete floor quicker, she just kept sapping the Emperor power into herself.

Amari's body went limp again, the gathering puddle of blood the only indicator that her heart was still beating.

Mackenzie didn't care much further than that. Rolling off Amari, releasing her hold on her limbs, she rolled on to the floor, uncaring as she sank to the concrete, the moisture of the blood seeping into the arm of her shirt. Her muscles buzzed as all the new magics tried to liven them, awakening her body – and yet the use it had already seen drained them enough that all she wanted to do was sink into the ground and escape the world right now.

She wanted rest.

Running steps sounded in the distance, but as she stared at the ceiling, adrenaline leaving her system and everything in her, feeling the weight of her exhaustion, Mackenzie couldn't find it in herself to move. It was over, and her battle had been "won", though she really didn't feel like it had. Not when after each altercation, the things to be grateful for seemed to shrink.

Matt's face came into view, peering down at Mackenzie, surveying her state. His eyes widened as he caught sight of the blood, his worry a comforting, genuine warmth that brushed against her mind.

"Are you hurt?" Matt asked hurriedly, leaning down beside her and offering his hand.

"Not physically," Mackenzie responded, taking it and letting him pull her to sitting, feeling the drip down her arm as she left the floor and blood behind. She was pulled to standing, shaky as she stood on her own legs again, but looked at Matt in time to see his sigh of relief.

"And Kai…?" he asked, his eyes drifting down the unconscious body behind her, one that she dared not look at for fear of falling apart.

"He's okay," she started, her voice cracking as tears threatened to overwhelm her. *God, I am so done with crying, when will it stop?* "If you consider forgetting about me okay… He has no injuries though."

"What happened?"

"He got the advantage and took her down… I… I tried to run so that he could keep it that way but she controlled me. The Devil tarot is immune to the Emperor's power because of the shapeshifting thing, so when she wasn't looking, he transferred the power to me," Mackenzie stammered, staring up at the dim downlights of her basement as the tears welled dangerously in her eyes, readying to escape. She needed to hold them back, to stay strong and not be upset *yet again*. She didn't dare look at Matt's face – which was no doubt dripping with pity – as his wave of sadness hit her.

"I'm so sorry, Mackenzie. But you got Amari to go down… That's something."

"I got her power too," Mackenzie said simply, focusing on the victory, not wanting to think about what she'd lost.

"You *what*? You got the Emperor power?" he asked, and she nodded in response, finally dropping her gaze from the ceiling as the tears subsided. "That's incredible! I know it may not feel like it right now but you have made a considerable dent in the Arcana's organization."

She nodded absent-mindedly as her gaze dropped down to Amari's body at her feet.

"If you need the Order to look after this mess, we can. That way you don't have to deal with the… aftermath," he said, his gaze flickering back and forth between the two unconscious people left behind by this battle.

It was an out she was all too relieved to hear and she

nodded quickly.

Matt reached into his pocket, pulling out his phone and texting someone – probably an Order member – before slipping it away and taking her arm lightly in his, uncaring of the bloodied sleeve. He led her away to the bottom of the stairs, wary not to let her turn back to the scene she was leaving behind, and guided her up the stairs, his touch soft and unassuming on her arm, his care and sympathy real and genuine.

If she couldn't feel the world ready to implode around her, she might have smiled. Instead she just followed, her face a smooth, neutral canvas, unable to be painted at the moment.

At the top of the basement stairs, he continued leading her up until they were on the landing of the second story. Letting go of her arm, he journeyed into the bathroom, leaving her standing there as she heard the tap for the bath begin to run.

With a furrowed brow – because that was as far as her emotions would let her delve into anything – she waited until he returned.

"We'll get you cleaned up," he explained.

She sank back on her heels, arms crossing over her chest as she looked at him with wide-eyes. Staring between him and the bathroom, she tried to figure out what his game was.

"I'm not hitting on you. I swear."

"So a bath in broad daylight?" she questioned.

"Would you prefer to stand up in the shower? Judging by the way you're standing right now, you're going to fall over in a few minutes if I make you shower. So a bath it is, and then I can keep an ear out in case you need help or try anything stupid," he explained.

She didn't respond, merely watching him curiously as he tried to talk his way through it.

"Just trust me. I put some of the lavender bath salts in there, so you have a lie in there, let your wounds heal and your body recover, and then when you get out, everything downstairs will have been taken care of. You've been through a lot in a matter of days – hours even. Just give yourself an hour to lie down in the water and ignore it."

She didn't have the fight to argue with him as she stood there, feeling the way her body swayed dangerously as though she were about to go tumbling down the stairs she stood mere feet from.

Matt took her arm again and guided her inside the bathroom, closing the lid on the toilet and getting her to sit on it as she waited for the water level to rise. He moved to the sink, kneeling in front of her as he took a warm cloth from the pile in her cabinet and began to dab at her neck, reminding her of the cut that still dwelled there.

Matt was quiet, his eyes not meeting hers as he worked to clean the cut on her neck carefully.

She watched his face, how intensely he focused as he worked. The thoughts that swirled around her were dangerous, upsetting to even have lingering over her head, but she feared what would happen if she left them to fester.

"I know what I have to do," she said simply, drawing Matt's confused and questioning gaze as he paused his wound-tending.

"What you have to do?"

"I have to take down the Major Arcana. For good. They can't be allowed to endure. I am going to hunt down every *single* one of them and take from them the powers that they don't deserve to have. That they have abused for years," she said confidently, feeling the surge of power in her as she voiced it. The other powers, the gold cuff bracelets, all seemed to fill her with magic at her own words, as though they were sentient and agreeing with the statement.

She waited for him to tell her it was an insane idea, or that she couldn't do it. If Kai had heard her say these things, he would've tried to talk her out of it, afraid of her getting hurt, but Matt just stared back at her, absorbing her words. He seemed to have no immediate objections to what she told him, or confusion as to why she felt the need to do so.

"It seems accurate and right that you were the one that prophecy spoke of."

"The prophecy?"

"The one descendant with true power in their heart that would reunite the Major Arcana in one person once again and return it to the way it had been?" he prompted, reminding her of something she'd heard before but never really paid much attention to.

"You don't seem surprised by me wanting to stop the Arcana," she observed, cocking her head to the side as she watched him.

"They aren't good people. I know that much and they're an organization that has been left unchecked, gaining power for too long. Just know that the Order of Wands will be here behind you to support you," he said with a surety she hadn't expected from someone she barely knew.

"Thank you," she said, her surprise hanging in the air between them. Despite all that she'd lost on her journey so far, she felt more sure of her purpose than ever before, and more determined that there was no going back to her life before.

She was the hunter of the tarot families now, and she had accepted her fate.

IT'S NOT OVER YET

This story is far from over!

Stay tuned for further updates by following along with Harley Jane Rose's social media and website.

ACKNOWLEDGMENTS

Sometimes I'm sure I could fill a book with how many people I want to thank for helping me on my writing journey. And with each new book comes a whole new list just as long as the last. Maybe one day I'll write a thank you book...

To start, thank you to the bookish community – my readers especially. I love it when you tell me your thoughts and it has been a dream come true to be able to share Mackenzie's story! Hopefully, I get to share many more stories with you that you'll feel as deeply as I do. Those of you I've met online through books and writing, I don't think I ever could have imagined the community I'd find and I'm so thankful I did. You are so supportive and I've made some amazing connections and looking forward to the oodles of ones yet to be found.

To those closer to home who are my cheerleaders, my honest truth-tellers, and my found (and blood) family, I cannot describe how much I appreciate you all.

My DC Fit dance family who have been there to support me, no matter what. In particular, *Steph*, who has read so many renditions of the Tarot Underworld books as I write them, and been my sounding board for all my ideas – good, bad, weird and stupid.

The other amazing women helping keep me on track, inspiring me to improve and grow my own character - and in turn - my stories, are *Laura, Tahlia and Renee* – you are some of my longest known chosen family and closest friends and I'm so glad, in our own ways, that I found each of you.

Ben. It feels weird to thank you in a book knowing how little time we've known each other in comparison to other people on this list but you have already impacted so much of my life that I'm not sure how I can't put you in here. You are a logical calming force to my chaos and someone I'm convinced stepped out of a fictional book just for me sometimes with how well you understand me, care for and complement my personality. You are a kind, generous soul I hope is destined to be in my journey a whole lot longer. Thank you.

And finally, *AMY LAURENS!* I am the writer – and woman – I am because of you. I don't think I would have reignited my spark and published my works – and attempted being an indie author - ever again if it hadn't been for you. You are a massive part of my life and have been a champion for my writing since you were my English teacher. Our lives have crossed so often, but I know it was all to help us shape each other in the most perfect ways at the right times.

Thank you will never sum up the gratitude I have for you.

And now I'm rambling in text form, so thank you to anyone who cared to read the whole way through this! I appreciate you!

ABOUT THE AUTHOR

Harley Jane Rose is a force to be reckoned with. Or – at least – she's trying to be.

Writing, reading, social media, dance, craft, and more. HJR is always striving to try what life has to offer. Those who know her will tell you, she is 0 or 100 with no in between, and the heart she gives to her stories is no exception.

Using inspiration from her life, travels, instinct, and inspirations, Harley Jane Rose's stories are psychological and heart-wrenching.

Keep an eye out for more tales that flirt with fantasy, romance, horror and more.

Milton Keynes UK
Ingram Content Group UK Ltd.
UKHW040836021124
450589UK00001B/59

9 780648 644545